"What . . . make love to a ghost?"

Marion's distress was overflowing. "Was I a hollow sham, a pathetic substitute for Andrea?"

"Marion!" Nicol shook her hard, eyes and voice dark with outrage. "Don't! I know how it must look to you, but you must understand. Let me come home with you now and give me the chance to explain to you. I kept telling you I had to talk to you, didn't I?"

"About my convenient resemblance to your late lamented wife? Oh, you kept saying it, but somehow you never quite got around to it, did you?" She gulped, and he saw how close she was to tears. "Not till you'd—"

"Until I'd what?" He was gruff now, eyelids heavy.

"Had what you were after!"

"I think," he stated with quiet deliberation, "we should go to your place and discuss this in private."

Rowan Kirby, happily married for eighteen years to an ex-research scientist, has two teenage children and lives near Bristol. With a degree in English, she has spent time teaching English to foreign students and has been involved in adult literacy. She always wanted to write, and has had articles published both in newspapers and in women's magazines. To date, six of her romance novels have been accepted by Harlequin. Her aim, she says, is to inject some new realism into the genre.

Books by Rowan Kirby

Don't miss any of our special offers. Write to us at the following address for information on our newest releases.

Harlequin Reader Service
901 Fuhrmann Blvd., P.O. Box 1397, Buffalo, NY 14240
Canadian address: P.O. Box 603,
Fort Erie, Ont. L2A 5X3

Shadow
Fall
Rowan Kirby

Harlequin Books

TORONTO • NEW YORK • LONDON
AMSTERDAM • PARIS • SYDNEY • HAMBURG
STOCKHOLM • ATHENS • TOKYO • MILAN

Original hardcover edition published in 1987
by Mills & Boon Limited

ISBN 0-373-02873-3

Harlequin Romance first edition November 1987

for
Deidre
(my favorite sister-in-law)
and every teacher in the world

CHAPTER ONE

'Now, today we're going to talk about some of the differences between all kinds of animals. For a start, who can tell me some things that are different about birds and fish?'

The sea of upturned faces was so familiar and friendly. Dark and fair, smiles and frowns, twenty-seven of them altogether with an average age of eight years, three months and five days.

Grouped round their tables in the bright classroom, they studied Marion with that air of collective expectancy which always drew her warmest response. Other people's children, but while they were at school, her children. She cared about each of them, their welfare and progress, personal as much as educational. And when she went home to her quiet flat in the evenings, she was still thinking about them, working their problems through. Partly because it was a good teacher's business to be involved in her pupils' problems; equally because that left Marion less time to face up to her own.

'Easy, Miss.' Jason got there first with a slick answer, as usual. 'Fish can swim and they can't fly. Birds can fly but they can't swim.'

'What about flying fish?' crowed Michelle, from the next table.

'Yeah, I saw a flying fish once,' her friend Diane endorsed. 'We was on this big ship and the fish flew out of the water and came on . . .'

'That wasn't *proper* flying.' Jason glared at them

7

both, mere girls as they were. 'That was a kind of—of jumping.'

'Ducks can swim.' Carrot-haired Timmy was thoughtful. 'And they're birds, aren't they, Miss?'

'That's not proper swimming.' Jason was going red in defence of his case. 'That's sort of floating. Not under the water.'

'Ducks do go under water!' Diane was no less indignant. 'They dive to get food. I've seen them at the park.'

'That's not what I meant.' Jason turned for support to Marion, who sat at the front watching and listening as she always did once a lively discussion got under way. 'You know what I mean, don't you, Miss? Tell them what I mean, Miss!'

He was a bright boy, but tense. She smiled gently at him. 'Of course I do, Jason. Fish are basically designed to live in water. Birds are made so that they breathe air, like us, but most of them are able to fly through it, too.' Jason made a triumphant face at his opponents. 'But then again,' Marion went on, 'it's also true that some birds can swim, and that some fish seem to fly short distances. We'll talk more about that in a minute. First, what about the other animals? The ones that walk on the ground? Can they fly? Can they swim?'

'I can swim three lengths,' announced Kevin proudly.

'You're not an animal,' Jason snapped.

'Yes, I am. People's a kind of animals, aren't they Miss?'

'No, they're not. People are people and animals are animals.' Jason was scornful.

'My dog's an animal, and he can swim brilliantly, so there!' Kevin stuck his tongue out at Jason.

Marion decided it was time to intervene, now things were getting personal. 'You're both right,' she soothed, but her dark eyes gleamed. 'People and dogs belong to the same family, really. We all have warm blood and we're called mammals. But when we say animals we don't always include humans. Okay, so what other differences can anyone think of?'

The silence was punctuated by giggles and whispers. 'I know, Miss,' little blond Dirk piped up, 'birds have feathers, and fish—fish have something else,' he subsided.

'Fish have scales,' Michelle informed him pompously.

'Very good, both of you.' Marion nodded. 'And what do you think the scales are there for? Anyone?'

'Keep 'em dry?' suggested Jason, never one to be outdone.

Before Marion could cut in on the burst of exaggerated laughter, worldly-wise Samantha Briggs spoke up from the sidelines. 'I read in my mum's paper about this boy who was covered in horrible black scales. Like a fish.' She paused for dramatic effect. 'When they tried to wash them off they just grew back, and they were all itchy, and he scratched them.'

This time the silence was rich with gruesome fascination as twenty-seven pairs of eyes, including Marion's, swivelled in Samantha's direction. She had captured her audience, and she knew it.

'Where did he live, then?' Jason was sceptical.

'What was his name? How old was he?' Diane was impressed.

'He lived in China, I think,' Samantha replied nonchalantly.

'Oh well, *China*!' Jason's tone implied that anything might happen in China, as long as it wasn't here in the real world of north London.

'My dad says you shouldn't believe everything you

read in the papers.' That contribution came from Mark, Jason's best friend.

'When I was in the launderette with my sister,' came another offering, from Timmy this time, 'I heard a lady say she knew a man who had one feather growing out of his back, and every time they pulled it out it grew again. One long feather,' he added, for extra impact. 'Like a—like a chicken.'

Marion was no less riveted than her charges by these outlandish tales, but it was time to bring this conversation back from the more far-fetched realms of fantasy to the cosy subject of nature study. Not that she was averse to a bit of fantasy, but she couldn't risk the children reporting to school in the mornings with bags under their eyes after suffering from nightmares. She knew how susceptible their imaginations were. 'I bet no one can think of an animal that breathes air like us, has warm blood, but lives in the sea?'

Several of them were ready for that one. 'Whales!'

'Well done. Any others?'

They looked at each other, then at her, shaking their heads. 'The Loch Ness Monster?' tried Jason hopefully.

'Loch Ness is a lake, not a sea,' Kevin was quick to show him up.

'Nothing like that, no. A real creature. Like a whale, only smaller,' Marion encouraged. The silence stretched and became restless, and she was on the point of breaking it when a small sweet voice from the back of the classroom rose and carried over to her.

'Dolphins?' It was softly hesitant, but clear.

Marion looked across at the far corner, as twenty-six heads turned to do the same. A steady blue gaze met theirs—veiled but quick, sharply intelligent. Marion's heart stirred and lifted. It was, it actually was, Rebecca Jarvis! New this term, tightly wrapped in the most impervious protective shell Marion had ever encountered in a child. Guarded, cautious; so far she had refused to join in any of these class free-for-alls Marion liked to orchestrate, but she took in every word, as was obvious from the quality of her written work. In school, these past few weeks, she had kept herself behind a screen, maintaining her privacy, withholding her trust, for reasons which Marion knew must go very deep but which she hadn't yet fathomed.

As she registered that pale pretty little face, the dark gold curls, the long thin features, Marion's smile widened. Then, enhancing the breakthrough of that one word spoken aloud in class, the girl smiled shyly back. A tantalising glimmer of sun through cloud, but enchanting; and reserved, Marion sensed, for herself alone.

Yes, it was a delightful moment, but Marion kept her reaction low-key and simply said: 'Absolutely right, Rebecca. Dolphins are mammals, like cats and dogs, cows and horses, and people of course. Have any of you ever seen one?'

Hands shot up, voices clamoured. 'At the safari park . . . we went to Whipsnade . . . I saw some in Brighton, in a big tank . . . on telly . . . they jump out of the water and laugh and catch things in their mouth . . .'

'Good, so you know all about them, then.' Marion tore her gaze from Rebecca's, allowing it to drift round the classroom. 'In a minute we'll see a picture of some. First I want one more big difference between birds, fish and mammals. What about the way they have their babies? Do we lay eggs?'

The lesson was rolling again. Marion was in charge, drawing out the shy ones, keeping the noisy ones under control, getting the best from everyone as far

as any teacher could. From the fringes, Rebecca
watched and listened intently, her eyes almost always
on Marion. The girl did not speak again, but the
teacher was aware of her acute absorption like a
thread stretched between them across the busy space.

After lunch Marion sat in the staff room with a pile
of exercise books and a cup of turgid coffee, trying to
breathe in as little of the fug as possible. Her
colleagues milled around, comparing notes on their
mornings, planning their afternoons. Marion avoided
looking up or catching anyone's eye. It was not that
she was particularly anti-social. Just that she currently
had good reason to shun close contact with the rest
of the staff.

In fact, considering the minor scandal she had
generated in that very room—almost a year of it, not
long ended—it was brave, some might say brazen, of
her to be there at all. Affairs between junior teachers
and deputy headmasters might not be unheard-of, but
they were packed with gossip potential. Lesser women
might have fled, given notice, found excuses to stay
away, but not Marion Thomas. She had Celtic fire to
match the glossy dark hair and spirited eyes. She had
determination, and above all she had total dedication
to her second-year Juniors at Burnbrook Primary. No
skirmish with any man, however desirable, and in the
bitter end however unsuitable, was going to deter
that instinct. On the contrary: after the crunch she
became more involved with 'her' children than ever,
seeking refuge in their unconsciously loyal support.

There had seemed such a future in it, way back in
that vibrant autumn term—was it really a whole year
ago? John Wood, with his sleek hair, suave suits, so
unusually groomed for a teacher. Charming, debonair,
he had captivated Marion far too easily, simply
because he was part of her own beloved reality:

school, the children. Not some escapist fantasy, beckoning her away to danger and threat, but a safe, integral piece of daily life. Or so she had thought, when he kept asking her to the pub for a drink after staff meetings, offering to drive her home, smiling and chatting so fluently, so attractively, until she could feel herself being gradually won over, pulled under his spell, though she fended the whole thing off as long as she could, keeping it securely on a business level.

But then it had felt quite natural when he had invited her out for a meal on one of those occasions, as they left the pub. Quite natural for her to accept. Quite natural for him to make the inevitable overtures in his car afterwards, and for her—warm-blooded, unattached as she was—to respond eagerly enough to them . . .

Now she gripped her red pen in tense fingers, scribbling viciously at a foolish mistake in the book on her lap. The flush on her cheekbones was of course due to the stuffiness in this room, with all the windows closed against the autumnal chill. This tendency to runny eyes was merely the result of all the cigarette smoke swirling around her. Marion felt irritated. It was disgusting the way so many of her colleagues indulged in the evil habit. Okay, so teaching could be a nerve-stretching occupation, but they were only harming themselves more—not to mention her—and worse, setting an appalling example to their pupils. John Wood had been one of the worst offenders, constantly on the point of giving it up but never quite making it. Typically full of grand intentions, but lacking the moral fibre to put them into action . . .

She should be grateful and relieved, of course, that she had found out the truth about him before it was too late; before any real damage had been done.

(Damage that went any further than her pride and
dignity, at least). She had actually got round to
inviting him over for a meal at her flat—just the two
of them, alone, off school premises, out of school
time, and even she could hardly pretend not to
understand where *that* might lead. He had accepted,
as if it was the most normal development in the
world, grinned suggestively at her, said how much he
was looking forward to it. Two days later she had
discovered, quite by chance, that he was married.

She cancelled the invitation, but she was no coward.
Instead, she insisted on meeting him at another local
pub, far from their usual haunts, and having the
matter out with him.

He was blithe and unashamed; evidently he had his
story ready. His marriage, he swore, was a dead
thing, seven years old and played out. His life was an
empty shell which only Marion could fill. His wife
had failed to understand him for years, being more
wrapped up in her own job than anything else. There
were no children. If Marion would give him time, let
him take it gently, he would make the clean break . . .
with her beside him, nothing was impossible.

Marion was attracted to him, and fond of him, and
now she was sorry for him. She agreed to wait, but
she did not renew the invitation to supper. Thank
heaven, she mused now, for small mercies and her
own firm principles! If it had been up to the persuasive
patter of John Wood . . .

As that spring term wore on, it grew increasingly
clear that he had never seriously intended to make
any sort of break, clean or otherwise. For him it had
been a kind of game—a diversion to boost an ailing
marriage. For Marion, it had been emotional reality:
part of everyday existence, her present and her future.
If the truth were told, she saw through him long
before the Easter holiday, but she clung to a shred of

pride and hope even after her feelings for him had dwindled.

Not long into the summer term, she had pulled herself together. All around her, tongues were wagging. The fact that they had no real cause made no difference at all. Rumour has little to do with fact, as Marion well knew. She took the situation in hand, refused to see John Wood again out of school, and made sure they met as seldom as possible in it. Under the smooth exterior, he was weak, recognising in Marion the stronger character who was not about to give way and embark on the harmless, spicy flirtation he had been after all along. He bowed out, and in deference to those wagging tongues, he handed in his resignation to the school governors. Doing the decent thing at last, and incidentally boosting his own career, he applied for a deputy headship at a larger school in another suburb—and got it. Gossip had it that he was already addressing his attentions to a fluffy young nursery assistant there.

Marion did not care whether that was true or not. She knew she was better off out of that relationship— if you could grace it with the description. Lonely, perhaps; hurt, certainly; but better off on her own, getting on with life as she had always done. She decided she was not cut out for all that emotional hassle; she was cut out to be an exceptional, devoted teacher. She had warm human company from the children, a few friends, a light, enjoyable social life. She should have realised the difficulty of being committed in two directions at once, mature woman of twenty-five as she was, not some impressionable girl fresh from college, dewy-eyed.

As usual, she spent the long summer holidays supervising groups of children at school camp. And now autumn was with them again, and everything had returned to its predictable flow.

Frowning now, she pushed back the curtain of black hair from her brow. She really must explain to Wayne for the umpteenth time why he shouldn't write in the margin. He was a dear lad, but slow . . .

'Hey, Marion!' Her head jerked up, her frown deepening, then disappearing. It was plump, cheerful Jilly, in charge of the reception class, now flopping down on the seat beside her. 'You look busy.'

'You look exhausted! What on earth have you been doing?'

'Nature ramble in the park.'

Marion nodded sympathetically. 'Say no more.'

Jilly sighed deeply. 'Why do we do it, Marion? Tracy Perks said she'd found some blackberries. I caught up in time to prevent them eating handfuls of the things. Whatever they were, they definitely weren't blackberries. Probably Deadly Nightshade. Remind me to look them up before next lesson.' She sighed again. 'And Dave Linton filled his pockets with slugs. What's his mother going to say this time? She won't have a chance to forget, either, because she's booked to come to the parents' evening tonight. She hasn't forgiven me for the incident with the matchbox full of worms. Are you all right, Marion?' She peered at her friend. 'Heavy morning?'

'Not really.' Marion smiled; she was fond of Jilly, and trusted her. 'I'm fine, and actually the morning was rather good. I think I might be making some headway with my new girl.'

'You mean Rebecca Whatsername?'

'Jarvis, yes. I think she might be emerging from her shell.'

'That's great. If anyone can do it, you can.' Jilly knew just how much it mattered to Marion. It mattered to them all, of course, but Marion took such an intense interest in her pupils. 'She's a clever kid, that one, but sort of cut off, isn't she? Strange.'

'She knows a remarkable amount, but she hardly says a word. Today she made a spoken contribution to the lesson. Short, but to the point. What's more, she smiled at me.' Marion smiled too, recalling it.

'She adores you, Marion. Everyone's noticed it. The way she keeps near you in Assembly, and stares at you when you're on playground or dinner duty. You're her lifeline, it's obvious.'

'She isn't exactly insecure; more sort of withdrawn,' Marion mused.

'An unusual kid. I heard she lives with an uncle and aunt. Is that right? What's her story?'

'That's the trouble, I'm not sure. Details are hard to come by. Her notes don't say much, and she says even less. I don't want to pump her, not in her present state. I gather she's lived abroad, and her parents are still in some far-flung corner of the globe. I'm sure this aunt and uncle do their best, but it can't be the same, can it? Plunging an eight-year-old into a new country, packing her off into a new family, just because it suits their convenience to go gadding . . .'

Marion pulled herself up short. Pointless to waste energy on airing these heartfelt opinions, when Jilly knew perfectly well how strongly she felt. And she was likely to need every ounce of energy tonight. Parents' evenings were notoriously hard going.

'Doesn't she mention her parents at all?' Jilly was genuinely concerned, but privately considered Marion's involvement went too far and too deep for her own good, if not that of the child.

'No. But I'm hoping to learn a bit more this evening. The uncle and aunt are booked to be there, I've just checked.'

'That shows willing, anyway. She's bound to miss her parents, but perhaps the uncle and aunt are doing their best.'

'It's not them I'm blaming.' Marion was grim. 'I'm

sure they're a tower of strength. No, it's the parents I'd like to meet. Give them a piece of my mind. Not that I'm likely to get the chance.'

'Just as well for them. We all know who'd get the best of *that* confrontation!' Jilly was half wry, half admiring. Marion's candour on such occasions was legendary. She leaned closer, changing tack. 'Hey, are your lot already getting themselves worked up about Christmas? Mine are. Isn't it dreadful, not half-way through October, and . . .'

'I know! It's ghastly.' That was another topic Marion felt strongly about, and she was successfully sidetracked. 'I try to keep their minds off it till late November at the earliest, but it's a struggle.'

'What are you doing this year?'

'Going to my parents as usual, I suppose. I hadn't thought.' Marion's reply lacked enthusiasm. 'What about you?'

'Oh, Brian and I have decided to stay put this year, just huddle together for warmth. He only gets three days, and anyway we're suffering from a severe acker-lacking condition. Stony broke,' Jilly translated, as Marion looked puzzled. 'I know they say Christmas is for families, but we prefer to hibernate and concentrate on each other for a few days. Forget the world, just be a cosy couple.' She grinned wickedly, then her face creased and she touched Marion on arm. 'God, I'm sorry! I didn't mean to say that. It was insensitive of me. I'm sorry, Marion.'

Her remorse was so tangible, Marion switched on her most reassuring smile. 'Don't be silly! I'll enjoy it. I expect my sister and brother will be there, complete with broods. It'll be fun.' But there was a tension in her voice. *Fun and games with the nieces and nephews. Plenty to keep good old Aunty Marion occupied. She's so marvellous with them, so natural with kids . . .*

The buzzer sounded for the first lesson. Saved by the bell, as teachers too often were. Marion bundled her books under one arm and slung her voluminous holdall over the other shoulder as she got to her feet. 'Must run, Jill. Got to pick up some worksheets from the Secretary's Office. Joan was photocopying them for me. See you.'

'Time for a quick cuppa at three-thirty, before the onslaught?'

'Good idea. I'll need fortifying, and the first customers aren't due till four-fifteen. I'll see you here then.'

'Have a good afternoon,' Jilly called, but Marion was already across the room. Jilly gazed after her for a few moments, half envying those long legs with their light purposeful step, the stylish grace of the dark red suede boots, the neat flared skirt swinging from shapely hips, the cable-stitched cream sweater nestling at the trim waist and emphasising generous curves, positive shoulders, straight back.

Then she shook her head, without malice or resignation. Marion did have all that, true, and she was excellent at her job. But she was so singular, alone in the world. Jill was short and dumpy and ordinary at most things, but she had Brian, and that was worth the rest put together.

The main hall bustled with dutiful teachers and eager parents. Marion sat behind her table, placed discreetly out of earshot of the next one. As she chatted confidently and competently to fond fathers and mothers about their precious offspring, she never lost sight of a pupil's individuality. She inspired approval and trust. No parent left her desk without a satisfied smile, even the ones whose children were causing or experiencing problems. Yes, indeed, she reflected, sardonic at her own expense: she was almost as

expert in the old public relations bit as she was at the
teaching itself.

Still, it was a long relentless task, keeping up this
calm, alert manner all evening. She rubbed her eyes
and glanced at her watch. Nearly seven: thank
goodness she was down to the last few names on her
list! Who hadn't she seen yet? Of course, the Jarvises.
Or just Mr Jarvis, it said here. That would be the
uncle; presumably the aunt had to stay at home with
Rebecca, perhaps had children of her own. Marion
was really looking forward to meeting this uncle,
filling in a few details, fleshing out the sad little
enigma that was Rebecca. No, sad wasn't quite the
right word. Subdued, that was nearer.

Here he came now, dead on time, homing in to sit
opposite her. But Marion had to finish the previous
pupil's notes, professional to her fingertips. Eventually
she looked up at him. Her reaction was powerful,
but completely controlled. What an extraordinary
resemblance! Amazing how family likenesses could
bypass the more direct relationships and emerge one
step removed. In this case, striking. This uncle was a
Jarvis, according to her file, so he had to be the
father's brother, and he certainly looked remarkably
like Rebecca.

It was a disconcerting echo, in a man probably
thirty years older, but she recognised that thin face
with the deeply defined features, full of character:
long straight nose, firm chin, and the gold-brown
hair, thickly waving. But where the little girl's skin
was smooth, pale, rather sallow, the man's was lined,
weathered; and where the child was slight and
ethereal, the man was lean but tough, in jeans and
cotton shirt. Not especially big, but wiry, compactly
muscular.

Sharp blue eyes scrutinised Marion from behind
metal-framed glasses. Her serene dark gaze levelled

back, registering everything, revealing as little as she could help. Unwittingly she had picked up a pencil and was playing with it, tapping the lead on the table.

'Miss Thomas?' The voice was as deep and sharp as the eyes, with a gritty quality, as if he were reproaching her for failure of concentration. His inspection of her was so quizzical, she felt marauded, exposed, but she was well used to not showing such responses.

'That's right, and you must be Mr Jarvis.' It was a statement, rather than a question. She stretched out her right hand, her smile coolly welcoming. He shook it, and his grasp was firm and dry. 'I'm glad to meet you. I'm hoping to learn more about Rebecca. She's an interesting child, but she worries me a bit.' Marion always came to the point; it saved so much time.

'Worries you?' His eyes narrowed, a faint undertone of hostility. His gaze was so intent, as if he was suspicious of what he saw; as if he wanted to penetrate below the surface to something underneath which perplexed him. Marion continued to study him in return, but she felt a ridiculous warmth, the beginnings of a heat, creep over her.

'A little. I wanted to ask you about her. Her situation.'

'Her situation?' It was little short of paranoid, the way he jumped on her words. What was biting the man? She was only his niece's schoolteacher, after all, nothing more significant than that. And they had barely exchanged two sentences.

'Her home situation. She's very bright, as I'm sure you know—outstanding, probably. Her homework is always good. But she's so quiet, withdrawn into herself. At school . . ..' He was watching her like a hawk. For a rare moment she floundered, then rallied. 'Mr Jarvis, please do tell me how she is at home, and whether she misses her parents a great deal? Does she talk to you and your wife about them? How long will they be away?'

Once started, the spate of questions seemed to flow of its own accord. He waited till she subsided, then leaned forward, brows arched with an air of faint surprise, hands flat on the table, palms down. They were fine hands, Marion noted automatically; tapering fingers.

'Miss Thomas, I'm not sure whether you've . . .'

But Marion was determined to have her say, and his words triggered hers off again. 'I must establish, before we go into her school record, what her background is, and especially what her feelings are about her parents, and living with you.' The man's frown had deepened, his brows all but meeting in the middle, but he allowed her to go on. 'All children need stability, and Rebecca's no exception.' Why was she gabbling, in the face of his steady stare? 'I'm sure you and your wife give her every support, but it's clear to me that she misses them at quite a profound level. If she cried or complained, it wouldn't be so bad, but she's so self-contained, so shut in . . .' Regaining confidence, Marion was scarcely aware how warmly her voice appealed and her dark eyes communicated. 'Tell me about your brother, Mr Jarvis. What does he do? When will he be back? Does he always take his wife?'

The man leaned back, folding his arms. The frown gave way to an ironic smile, twisting slightly sideways. The eyes flashed real amusement, in among the mixture of attack and defence.

Then it was his turn to bend towards her, hands linked under chin, expression curiously blank. 'Miss Thomas, I rather think we have to clear up a small misunderstanding before we go any further. And before you allow any more of that blatant disapproval to spill out of its professional packaging. You're doing a grand job so far at hiding it, but I'm not blind nor deaf. I think you might regret it if I don't put you in the picture.'

'That's what I *want* you to do,' she pointed out, alarmed and annoyed by his words as well as his manner.

'For a start,' he explained calmly, his eyes never leaving her face, 'it's not my brother you're so eager to hear about.'

'It's not?' She blinked, taken aback.

'I think not, Miss Thomas.'

'Then who is it?' she demanded suspiciously.

'It's me. I'm not Becky's uncle.'

'You're not?' But she knew exactly what he was going to say.

Her intuition was right, and with it came a surge of discomfort. 'I'm afraid not.' He leaned nearer, and there was a spark of humour in the lucid eyes behind their lenses. 'I'm her father.'

CHAPTER TWO

'OF COURSE you're Rebecca's father.' Marion nodded, as if she had known all along; and at some level, surely she had.

All the same, she moved back in her chair, out of his range. He still watched her carefully—more interested, even inquisitive, than he had any right to be.

'Rebecca has been living . . . staying,' he amended brusquely, 'with her Uncle Denham and his wife Frances. I'm the elder brother,' he explained. 'The returned prodigal, it would seem,' he added drily. 'Nicol Jarvis, yours to command.' He said this with a short, sharp bow of the head, satirically theatrical like a swashbuckling hero from a period drama.

'I see.' Marion only wished she did. 'Well, I'm glad to know you're back, Mr Jarvis, because . . .'

'Because you've been worried about Becky,' he cut in rudely. 'Yes, you've made that clear. Can you be more specific, Miss Thomas?'

'I was just about to, Mr Jarvis,' she retorted instantly, coldly meeting his stare. But how tricky it was, at the best of times, sorting out the more complex problems associated with her pupils in these brief formal sessions, when the atmosphere was so public!

'Then I apologise for interrupting you.' Disarmingly he had softened his tone, and now leaned back expectantly. It was a bit like being confronted with an unpredictable wind, gusting now this way and now that, but always overwhelming.

Marion collected herself, ready to begin again, take up the reins. 'Since your daughter joined us a few weeks ago, I've had plenty of opportunity to observe her, get to know her. I'm responsible for most of her lessons. It's only natural she should have formed some attachment to me, under the circumstances, but I get the impression that in her case this attachment might go deeper than usual. She hardly speaks, but she does choose to join me even when there's no need—at break, for instance, or dinner, when I'm on duty.'

'I'm not at all surprised.'

Marion glanced up at this cryptic comment, but refused to allow her flow to be diverted. She was used to dealing with every variety of difficult doting parent; she wasn't about to start being daunted by one now. 'Teaching Rebecca is a pleasure because she's so receptive, but . . .' she paused, not for effect but to choose her words carefully.

He was into the gap like a whiplash. 'But?'

Again Marion ignored the tense challenge. 'She's so solemn. She seems shut away, inside herself. She listens, but she won't join in with the group. She prefers to work and play on her own. She's made no real friends, not that the other children don't want to socialise with her, more as if she keeps them at bay. In lessons I know she's taken things in, because her written work is excellent, but she hardly ever contributes. I always encourage active participation from my pupils, and I've tried several approaches—involving her, leaving her alone—it's always the same. She understands, fast and accurately. She produces lovely homework—imaginative, thoughtful.'

'Hmm.' The father was following all this, his brow

creased. Now he smiled slightly. 'She always did have a vivid imagination.'

'But she's so locked in. It's as if we can't reach her . . . she doesn't want to be reached.' Marion had said her say; now she waited.

Nicol Jarvis gave little away: not overtly hostile, not entirely sympathetic. 'So, you think she's deeply unhappy?'

It was a common enough ploy, fielding her own questions back at her. 'Not exactly unhappy. More . . .' she deliberated. It was vital to get these things just right. 'Uncertain. Defeated. Almost . . .' she hesitated again, 'bruised.'

'Once bitten.' Marion decided to let this muttered private reflection pass, and simply waited for his further reaction. 'So what do you want me to do about it, Miss Thomas?' he snapped.

Marion sighed. It could have gone either way with a man as intelligent as this, and he had opted for the defensive. Pity—that was so potentially negative. She willed herself to stay detached and in charge, but it was impossible to force the concern out of her tone. 'First of all, you can tell me about Rebecca's home life, her experience. I gather you've been away and left her with this uncle and aunt. In my estimation she's suffering from a sense of loss. The classic childhood enemy, insecurity. They all need . . .'

'Stability. So you've already pointed out,' he interrupted acidly. His gaze had never left her face, and she was beginning to feel exhausted with the effort of honest, unruffled communication. 'I can see that you have my daughter's best interests at heart. Den and Fran did say this had the reputation of being a good school, and clearly they were right. I came here this evening with the intention of finding out for myself.'

And not before time. But Marion kept her sarcastic

reaction quiet, simply repeating, 'So, what can you tell me?'

He studied her with a calm clarity. Then, disconcertingly, he looked down at his watch. She noticed that he wore it unconventionally on the inside of his right wrist, and that the skin there was richly tanned and covered with dark-gold curling hairs. 'According to the *billet-doux* I received from your school secretary, our strict allocation is a quarter of an hour, and that was up three minutes ago. There's no way I can enlighten you about Becky in minus three minutes.' He glanced over his shoulder to where another couple waited patiently at a tactful distance. 'Also, I think you have some more customers.'

Damn, how unlike her, how unprofessional, not to have kept this interview well under control, not to have noted the time! But Marion smiled across at the other parents to show she had not forgotten them, replying crisply, 'Yes, one more pair after these. They won't mind waiting a few minutes, Mr Jarvis, if you could be brief.'

'I'm sure they won't mind waiting,' he agreed blandly. 'But I do mind being brief. If I'm going to fill you in on Becky's situation, I'd rather do it in confidence and at leisure.' His mouth and tone had both tightened, grim, intimidating. Suddenly he was bending towards her, hands once again resting on the table. 'What time do you escape from this jamboree, Miss Thomas?' he demanded abruptly.

She was shocked into equal directness. 'I should be off by eight.'

'What do you do after that?'

'Nothing. That is, I was going home, having something to eat and . . .'

'No one expecting you? No unbreakable engagements?'

His tactics were so uncompromising, they effectively

dampened her righteous indignation even before it
could stir. 'No,' she admitted.

'Then meet me afterwards for a drink, and I'll put
you in the picture.'

He sat back, ran an expansive hand through his
already unruly hair, and regarded her with mingled
defiance and humour. Marion considered, but only
for a second. Dignified objectivity mattered, of
course—but so did her determination to get to the
root of a pupil's problems. The two were not mutually
exclusive. And she believed in following hunches,
true to her Celtic temperament. For Becky's sake,
instinct led her to accept his invitation and the
challenge behind it.

'Certainly.' Her smile was all charm and poise now.
'Where?'

'Good.' He, in turn, registered no more than a
flicker of surprise. 'Do you know Gino's? Italian
place on Station Road?

'Of course. I go there quite a lot.'

'Right. I'll be there, from eight. Okay?' He stood
up.

'Okay. I'll join you when I can.'

'No rush. Mustn't short-change your other grateful
clients on my account.' He grinned, turned and strode
off across the hall, a jaunty figure, no more than
averagely tall but exuding a tangible air of male
confidence.

Marion watched until he was out of sight, then
pulled her attention back to the job in hand. 'Mr and
Mrs Bartlett?' she called pleasantly. 'Do please come
over. I'm sorry to have kept you.'

While they made their way to her desk, Marion's
pen hovered above her notes. She was supposed to
record the upshot of the Jarvis interview, but really,
there was nothing much to write, except that the
father had duly attended. She ticked the narrow

column next to Rebecca's name. No, there was
nothing more she could usefully add by way of
background information; not yet.

So why was there this sensation of having actually
communicated with a person for once, instead of the
usual polite superficial noises? She had found out
little enough. Not even, she realised with a jolt,
anything about the child's mother. Nicol Jarvis's
wife. Nicol: an uncommon name, for an evidently
uncommon man.

She pushed Rebecca's folder to the bottom of the
pile. Time to add a few details later, when she had
learned them.

Nicol's glance encompassed the scene. The popular
trattoria and wine bar, already filling up for the
evening; wax-coated Chianti bottles, candlelight soft
on red tablecloths, paintings on the walls: Venice,
Florence, Naples, Rome. Guitars providing lyrical
atmosphere through hidden loudspeakers. *O Sole
Mio* . . .

He poured a glass from his carafe of house red,
and half-drained it. Irony sparked in his acute blue
eyes, but a measure of appreciation too. Not such a
bad little dive, considering it was a few points north-
west of Finchley on the Northern Line. It really tried,
and on the whole it succeeded. He smiled as he
compared it with some of the more exotic haunts
he'd patronised. Sleazy dens, sumptuous nightclubs,
in Bangkok, Singapore, Yokohama; or more recently
Veracruz, New Orleans, Guatemala . . .

He shook his head, frowning as he narrowed his
gaze on the door. Eight-thirty, and where was this
woman? He'd told her not to rush, but he couldn't
wait all night. It was already a bit late to get back
in time to tuck Becky up. And what was he
playing at anyway, arranging trysts with prim

schoolmistresses when he had better things to do
with his time?

He sighed. No, this was important; nothing was
more important than his daughter's welfare. Maybe
he should order this Miss Thomas a drink. What
tipple did self-contained young spinsters of this
parish prefer? Sweet sherry? A nice drop of German
white? He'd better wait till she appeared. She
looked like the sort who knew her own mind, and
who might just get touchy if decisions were made
on her behalf. Especially by men. He was a fair
judge of human nature, and he recognized the
signs.

His left hand tightened round the glass, while his
right ran automatically through the thickness of his
hair. Just as well Becky's teacher showed evidence
of a strong character. Apparently she was going to
need it, what with Becky . . .

At last, here she was now, an outdoor jacket
over that rather fetching sweater, bag slung from
one of those neat shoulders, making her way straight
towards him between the tables. He half stood as
she reached his corner and sat opposite him without
preamble, shedding her jacket on to the back of her
chair, flicking the rich dark hair off her face and
regarding him through those direct brown eyes.

'Miss Thomas; thanks for coming.' His chivalry
was partly natural, partly studied.

'Why wouldn't I come? I said I'd be here. Didn't
you believe me?'

'Of course I did. Just that you must be pretty
well fed up with the sight of fond parents tonight. I
mean, the problems of one's own dear offspring are
one thing, but you must wish you could leave your
pupils' little foibles behind you after a hard day's
teaching?'

Her stare was not without an edge of steel. 'Mr

Jarvis, my concern for my pupils goes deeper than that. Any help or support I can give, any way I can understand them better, add to their school personalities, I make it my business to do so.'

'I'd better believe it,' Nicol murmured, but respect leavened the amusement in his eyes. Then he became brisk. 'Right. Well, the least I can do, under the circumstances, is provide some sustenance. What can I offer you, Miss Thomas? They do a good selection of wines, all the usual aperitifs, or I'm sure they'd concoct you one of those syrupy cocktails if that's your fancy.' His expression showed his personal distaste at the last idea. 'Shall we see the list?'

'What's that you're drinking?'

'A rather good Rosso. Full-bodied, quite rough, the way I like them. But it packs a fair punch, so please don't think you have to . . .

'That's what I'd like.' Marion was decisive. 'And a Mozzarella pizza with a side salad, if it's not too much trouble. They do a good one here, and I'm starving.'

Nicol was both impressed and disconcerted, but he displayed neither. A woman who relished her food and wasn't afraid to say so; a woman who shared his taste in dry red vino; things were looking distinctly encouraging. Clearly, Becky was in capable hands.

'It shall be done.' He went over to the counter to order two pizzas, returning with a second glass and a small bowl of olives. 'Help yourself, Miss Thomas. The food won't be long.'

Marion was already pouring herself some wine, without waiting for him to do the honours. She seemed oblivious to his gaze, intensifying on her as she sipped, then leaned back to smile at him. 'That's better!'

'Been a tough evening's consulting?' He was almost sympathetic.

'Not particularly. Nothing I couldn't cope with. Just long.' She covered a yawn, then took another sip. 'Now, let's hear about Rebecca.' Again, no beating about the bush. 'I want to know why she's like she is, what makes her tick. Otherwise there's very little I can do to help bring her out of this shell, or whatever she's in.'

He took an olive and bit into its succulent flesh. 'I think I'd better start by telling you something about myself.'

'That's often the best way.' He watched her soft lips, unmade-up, as she placed an olive between them, chewed it, took the stone delicately in finger and thumb and put it in the ashtray. She was socially assured; far from the graceless schoolma'am. He, of all people, ought to have known better than to judge by preconceptions, or appearances, or . . .

He swigged some wine, calling himself to order. 'As you've gathered, I travel a lot.'

'I gathered you'd been away, of course. Rebecca's notes . . .'

'I wanted to ask you about them.' He was animated suddenly, clunking his glass down on the table as he bent towards her. 'Just what does it say about all this in Becky's official file? The one you had on your desk?'

Marion laughed. 'Don't worry, there's nothing sinister. Every pupil has one. It's standard practice in most local education authorities.'

'Yes, yes, fair enough.' He waved a hand, mildly irritated. 'But what does it *say*?'

'Something extremely uninformative, like 'parents abroad', and that she lives with her aunt and uncle, Mr and Mrs Jarvis.'

'I suppose that's a start.' He drew in a long

breath as if preparing for action, and Marion was
alerted. 'The first point to clear up is this matter of
'parents'. Obviously there's been a communications
block.'

Marion's brow wrinkled. 'How do you mean?'

Before Nicol could reply, there was a call from
the counter that their pizzas were ready, and he
marched across to fetch them. As soon as he set
hers down on the table, Marion picked up her knife
and fork, but without letting the subject slip. 'What
did you mean, "parents"?'

'Becky does not have parents. She has a parent.'
That was succinct enough; if she could be direct, so
could he. He started on his pizza.

Marion had stopped eating, her whole attention
focused on him. 'You mean . . .'

'I mean my wife is dead.'

'Oh no!' It was her turn to scrutinise him, but she
showed no embarrassment, only concern and horror.
He was accustomed to putting up every protective
layer when this topic was aired, but something in
this woman's genuine, intelligent compassion seeped
through the barriers.

She said no more, simply waiting until he was
ready to continue. 'It was an accident, two years
ago. We were in Hong Kong at the time.'

'What happened?' She allowed herself a gentle
prod as he fell silent.

'Happened?' His gaze had turned inwards. Marion
understood that he had to recite these events like a
rehearsed tract. Never mind whether or not she
knew of the places, the people—this was the only
way he could clothe such a tragedy in words, even
now. 'She was on a launch picnic. They sailed to
one of the more remote islands. They moored in a
small bay, off Lantau, and a freak tropical storm
blew up. We had a bit of warning, but not enough

to catch them; their radio equipment was switched
off and the emergency signals came through very
suddenly.'

He paused, and when he resumed the tale his
voice had lost that chanting, intoning quality and
his eyes were clear on hers again. 'You get that
there, in high summer, Miss Thomas. A typhoon
will lurk in one area, then change direction in
minutes and whip across to another.'

He paused again, and again Marion prompted,
'You and Rebecca weren't with her? You didn't go
on the picnic?'

'She went with other friends. No, we weren't in
the party.' He had become deadpan again, and now
he hacked off a large piece of pizza. 'The boat was
dashed against some jagged rocks. They found the
bits of it later. Fancy job, it was,' he added grimly,
'all mod cons, but that didn't prevent it being sliced
up.'

'Oh God!' The vision was so vivid, and his distress
so candid, how could anyone fail to be moved?
'Were they all . . .?'

'They were drowned—everyone on board. The
bodies were washed up next day, on a beach not far
away.'

The way he stated these bare facts was so cruel
and bleak, Marion surged with a violent need to
deflect the recalled drama, return to the present.
'What about Rebecca?' She forced herself to sound
calm and steady. They were here to discuss the
effects of this disaster on the child, after all.

'What about her?' Reliving the anguish lent
gruffness to his tone.

'She—reacted badly?' It sounded silly. Of course
she would react badly. What child wouldn't?

'Badly?' He shrugged, as if surprised. 'Not really.
She never saw a great deal of Andrea, as it happens.

My wife was keen on the more sophisticated aspects of colonial life,' he explained dully. 'The glitz, the glamour. There's plenty of that on offer out there, as you're doubtless aware.' *It's not exactly my scene*, his expression implied.

'I've heard about it.' Marion was cautious, but intrigued. 'I've hardly travelled at all,' she volunteered, willing him to carry on.

Nicol had regained his composure. 'Of course Becky missed her mother. But she'd had the same *amah* since we arrived there. Nanny,' he translated, but Marion was already nodding to show that she knew the term. 'She went on with her life, going to primary school, seeing her friends. And she had me. We'd always been close.' An unexpected smile lit the lean face, crinkled the blue eyes. 'Last June, I finished the work I was there to do, and we came back here. I suppose that was when she started to become—withdrawn, as you so aptly put it.'

'Delayed reaction?' Marion suggested, as he tailed off again.

'The new environment. Settling in with my brother and his wife. Knowing I had to go off again, without her this time.' He grew abrasive, probably in self-defence. 'I really couldn't have her with me, Miss Thomas, not where I was going. Moving about all the time . . . no one to look after her . . . it seemed best all round if she stayed with Frances and Denham. I said I'd come back as soon as I could, stay as long as I can, and that's what I'm doing.' He took off his glasses, rubbed his eyes with forefinger and thumb. Marion noticed the shadow of weariness across the weathered complexion and clear gaze.

It was time to broaden the picture, take the pressure off the man—find out more details for her file. 'Why do you travel, Mr Jarvis? What do you do? Military? Diplomatic?'

He glanced up sharply, smiling slightly at her guesswork. Or perhaps her question had struck him as out of place? 'The name is Nicol. I have a particular dislike of standing on ceremony. Or is it against professional etiquette?' He was shrewd, noting her conflicting response. 'Not done, between parents and teachers? Threat to discipline?'

'Whose discipline—theirs or ours?' she countered at once. She returned his smile, alleviating the tension, but she did not return his invitation.

Nicol pushed his plate aside. 'No, Miss Thomas.' He underlined her surname with a trace of satire. 'I'm neither a member of Her Majesty's armed forces, nor one of her political representatives overseas. I'm a humble scholar, a practical academic. A social anthropologist by trade, though in recent years I've spread my net wider to include local history, ethnic research, environmental studies. I've written several tomes, on several parts of the world, which several million people have been kind enough to buy, thus enabling me to carry on this peripatetic lifestyle. Which suits me fine, and suited Andrea, but . . .'

'But doesn't necessarily work out so well for Rebecca,' Marion supplied, as he faltered, staring down into his wine glass. 'Did your wife always go with you?' she persisted.

'Lord, yes. She'd never have missed a minute of it. Lived life to the full, did Andrea.'

Marion detected his bitterness, and put it down to a natural sense of loss. Two years wasn't so long, and to lose your partner to the relentless clutches of the ocean . . .

She laid down her knife and fork, and tried once

more. 'If Rebecca wasn't devastated at the time, do you think she . . .'

This time Nicol co-operated. 'Let me go back to square one. Becky was born eight years ago in New Delhi, when I was engaged on my first major project, on the Indian sub-continent. Then we came to England for a couple of years while I wrote it up. After that it was the Far East. I'd always wanted to study some of the different cultures there, and that first book did so well, my publishers advanced me enough to fulfil that ambition. While we were there, Andrea . . .'

Marion nodded to show she was with him and he need not spell it out. 'I stayed on to write the book,' he declared tersely. 'And Becky stayed on with me, of course. Then I got this current commission. It'll be a shorter piece this time, for an international publication—based on the original races of Central America; what remains of them now, in terms of people, places, artefacts, records . . . myths and legends, archaeological evidence . . . fascinating stuff, Miss Thomas.'

'I'm sure.' The way he described it, anything would be.

He was leaning towards Marion as if ready to pre-empt her criticism. 'I don't want to leave Becky, but I do have a living to earn,' he pointed out urgently. 'And this is what I do best—what I feel called to do. I thought of finding a boarding school, but surely an affectionate uncle and aunt—two little cousins . . .?'

'Of course that's better than boarding school.' Marion was able to be magnanimous, and on this point she was vehement. 'How old are the cousins? They're not at Burnbrook, are they?'

'Not yet. They're no more than babies. Future customers, I dare say.' He grinned, then was serious again. 'Becky adores them, and she gets on fine with Frances and Den too, I can assure you. I'd never have left her with them otherwise, and they'd have had more sense than to take her on,' he added as an afterthought.

'I can see that.' Marion knew her judgment had been hasty; typically impetuous. She should have waited to learn the background. Good thing she was always so restrained, on the surface, and had managed not to disgrace herself on meeting the man by losing her temper. 'And your brother—is he in the same line as you?'

Nicol's grin was wider this time. 'God, no!' He laughed outright, as if at a private joke. 'Den's a man of the cloth. The Reverend Denham Jarvis, vicar of St Peter's. A thoroughly good man, and a truly wise one, in my opinion. Unlike his errant sibling.'

'The prodigal brother?' Marion returned the grin, remembering. 'Mr Jarvis, I'm sure they'll do their best for Rebecca, and so will I. From what you've told me, it's not surprising she's suffering from a certain—what shall we say?—dislocation.' It was time to choose her phrases with care and efficiency, drawing on her wealth of humanity and experience. 'Postponed shock is always on the cards, in fact considering everything I'd say she was doing very well. Now that I understand, it'll be much easier to help. I only wish we'd known all this from the beginning.'

'It wasn't censored.' Nicol was watching her closely as she made her statement. 'Obviously a case of every party assuming the other party had genned up the authorities,' he speculated drily. 'Classic.'

'I can see you had no choice, if your research

takes you to far-flung spots like—where did you say? Central America?'

'I was there last week,' he confirmed. 'Strange thought, isn't it?'

'Peculiar.' Marion's imagination was gripped. She'd never been further than Brittany herself, and that was just a short holiday. It must be great, she found herself reflecting wistfully, to wander freely among such settings, and be handsomely rewarded for it into the bargain. He was a clever man, evidently; a man of sharp observation and a quick mind. An ability to assimilate data and set it out so that ordinary folk would enjoy reading it. Ordinary folk like her, stuck in their humdrum lives, plodding routines.

People like Nicol Jarvis provided education even to the educators, an extra breadth of insight. Not only that, they brought fantasy—vicarious excitement, a gloss to the tarnished daily grind, and that was probably even more valuable. He deserved his success. And now here he was, drinking with her in an unpretentious wine bar on the fringes of this great city which was home to her and millions of others.

Then again, it was foreign, perhaps even glamorous, to someone, somewhere else in the world. A pleasing thought, which had never hit her before.

Marion tuned in on Nicol's enthusiastic account of his work. 'Last week,' he was elaborating, 'I was in Mexico City, browsing in the archives. We can still learn an amazing amount from those ancient Indian tribes—the Aztecs, the Incas, the Mayas. Even today, their descendants have some totally different ways of looking at life. I was telling Fran this, only this morning.'

He rested both elbows on the table top, fingers linked, eyes unwavering on Marion's. 'Here's an example, Miss Thomas. If you wanted to describe, in physical terms, a person contemplating their past or their future, how would you express it? Which way would you picture them facing?'

It was infectious, his eagerness. Marion deliberated, then replied, 'I'd say they looked back over their past, forward to the future.'

'Exactly!' His laugh was almost a crow of triumph. 'So would I. But you know how a Mayan Indian would see it?' She shook her head, aware that she was as riveted by the man himself as by what he was telling her. 'To them, it's obvious that we look ahead to the past, because we can see what's happened along the road. According to them, the future must be behind us, or we'd be able to see it clearly.'

'That really makes sense!' There was a delight, almost an elation, in Marion's response. How satisfying—how strangely logical, yet how alien—to be granted such a glimpse into another culture's way of perceiving reality!

Her pleasure reflected his. 'It certainly does, and so do many of their attitudes, once you learn to accept them. If they'd been able to develop, those civilisations could have taught ours a thing or two. Still can, as I say. Don't you think so, Miss Thomas?'

'Marion.' It was spontaneous, a correction and more, as if some inner reserve had been suddenly stripped away.

Nicol smiled very slightly, but he went on. 'What I'm over there to find out is just how much we can learn from them today. It'll take me a bit longer yet. I've already been there since August, and I have to go back soon—but I'll do all the writing up in London this time.' Again it was as if he anticipated Marion's complaints on Rebecca's behalf.

'I can't leave the job half done. And I couldn't turn up this opportunity, could I, Marion?'

His voice rose and hardened as he spoke her name for the first time. He had put his case, deliberately won her over, and she conceded a victory to him, though it was an obscure one, hard to define. Normally she might have struggled, but this time that would only have compounded her defeat. As things were, part of the achievement seemed to be hers too.

Her mind was working at top speed. The Mayas weren't the only ones capable of revealing new approaches to life. Marion Thomas, in north London in the nineteen-eighties, was far from bogged down or blinkered.

'Could I, Marion?' Nicol repeated his demand, more emphatically, into the silence.

'No, Nicol, you couldn't. Rebecca must take her chance, along with the rest of us. We'll all do what we can to see that things run smoothly for her. I'll have to fill my colleagues in on some of this, for the record; I hope that's all right with you?'

'I trust you to do what's best for the kid, Marion. I wanted to paint the full picture, and that's why I suggested we meet here.' His smile was wry. 'You can see now that it wouldn't have been on, cramming all that into minus three minutes, surrounded by staff and parents. I don't go in for expecting special treatment, but in this case . . .'

'In this case you were fully justified, and I'm glad you asked me.' Marion was already withdrawing from the rare contact, putting her guards up; quite enough real communication for one day. 'Now you must excuse me, I've got to get home. If I could just settle up with you for the food and drink.' She opened her purse, businesslike.

'Certainly not!' The gold-brown brows arched,

outraged. 'I know all about equality, but I was the one who dragged you here, and I insist on providing the refreshments, at the very least.'

Marion accepted with a good grace. 'Thanks.' She stood up, reaching for her jacket. 'I needed it, and I appreciate it.'

He was on his feet beside her, helping her on with the jacket. His knuckle brushed her nape, cool on the smooth warmth of her skin. To dissipate her fierce awareness of the touch, she disentangled her hair from inside her collar and shook it out around her face, an automatic gesture, probably repeated a dozen times a week. Then she turned and walked ahead.

'Can I give you a lift, or do you have a car?' He was a step behind.

'I don't drive, but I only live round the corner, thanks all the same.' Outside she swung round to smile at him, poised once more.

'We'll keep in touch, then, Marion. About Becky.'

'Fine.' There was no awkwardness, just a rather studied detachment. Not so difficult, out here on the damp street instead of in that cocoon of spurious intimacy, back there in the trattoria. 'I'm sure your brother and his wife would let me know if there was any particular problem.'

'I'll make sure they do. I'll be around a couple of weeks yet. You might notice some improvement in Becky, even in that short time.'

'Actually, I did think there was a loosening up, only today . . .' Marion became thoughtful. 'She made a real contribution to a lesson. It was about dolphins.'

'Dolphins?' He blinked, then chuckled. 'Oh, she's seen dolphins! The real thing, in the South China Sea. Knows all about them.'

'That would explain it.' Marion thrust her hands

into the pockets of her jacket. The evenings were drawing in, growing chill. 'I must go, Mr Jarvis.' Suddenly she felt cold and exposed and painfully tired.

'Nicol,' he reminded her softly, moving a step closer, holding out a hand. His left hand, she noticed; she had registered it subliminally, as he ate—that he was left-handed, like his daughter. Interesting.

Laughing at himself, he substituted his right one. 'Social mores do not cater for aberrants like Becky and me. Hereditary, do you think, Marion? Learned, or genetic?'

'You're the expert in anthropology.' She shook the offered hand firmly. 'I'll see you again, I expect, Nicol. Thanks again. Goodbye.'

Then she was walking away, leaving him alone on the pavement; carrying off an image of light from Gino's curtained windows picking out the gold threads in his hair.

'Goodbye, Marion.' He watched her receding figure, shapely, purposeful. She reached the corner and disappeared round it without looking back. Immediately he set off briskly in the opposite direction, to where he had parked his hired car, half a block away.

CHAPTER THREE

IT was noticeable right from the next morning. Rebecca had begun to open out like petals on a tight bud, disclosing the true bright colours inside. The effortless miracle had been achieved by having her father home again, of course, but Marion allowed herself a small corner of credit too.

There was such a satisfaction in watching this child blossom before her keen eyes. The cautious smiles spread to generous grins, most often aimed in Marion's direction but increasingly elsewhere as well. That single-word contribution to a lesson grew gradually into short sentences, then several at once. She even started responding tentatively to the other children's cheery advances, though it was still early days to expect her to put out her own feelers.

Marion rejoiced silently, knowing she was seeing a glimpse of the real Rebecca at last, the one who had been locked up, defended and protected from the outside world, but now showed herself a little more confidently each day. It was a joy and a fulfilment. It was what this job was all about.

The improvement continued the rest of that week, and the first half of the next. Then Rebecca disappeared—or at least, she did not come to school. Wednesday and Thursday went by, with no sign of her. On Friday, there was still none. Marion was alarmed at her own reaction. The gap left by the Jarvis girl in the classroom seemed to extend to other parts of her, where it had no business to be.

After school on Friday, Marion gave way to an uncharacteristic panic. She looked up the Jarvis telephone number in her file, went straight to the empty Secretary's Office, and dialled it before she could change her mind. Her stomach felt uneasily clenched, as if more was at stake than a routine enquiry after a missing pupil.

'Hallo?' It was a pleasant female voice, rather breathless.

'Er—Mrs Jarvis?'

'Frances, yes. Can I help you?' She was the vicar's wife, Marion reminded herself: a profession in itself, supportive, efficient, caring. Not unlike being a teacher, in a way.

'This is Marion Thomas, Rebecca's teacher at Burnbrook. I was . . .'

'Miss Thomas! Good heavens! We've heard such a lot about you!'

'Oh.' Marion was briefly nonplussed. 'Have you?'

'Yes. Becky never stops going on about you—Miss Thomas this and Miss Thomas that. You're a palpable hit, I can tell you.'

'How boring for you!' Marion's irony was directed mainly at herself. For a moment there, her thoughts had flown to Nicol rather than his daughter, though why on earth he should have talked about her . . . 'We get on fine, Rebecca and I.' She knew she sounded at her most clipped and formal, but there was an exposure to cover up. 'And I've noticed how much better she's been feeling recently, so . . .'

'Yes—that's because her father's been back,' Frances pointed out warmly. 'We did our best for her, naturally, but she was bound to miss Nicol. She's never been without him for long, you see. Especially since . . . anyway, Miss Thomas,' Frances assured Marion earnestly, 'she was always happy to go off to

school, and calm when she got back, and we know
we've got you to thank for that.'

'Ah, well, I'm glad if I . . .' Somehow Marion was
losing her initiative.

'Yes, and that made it all the more annoying when
she went down with this bug. Just as she was really
settling in. A real drag.'

Marion seized the opportunity to get to the point.
'That's why I'm phoning, actually. To find out why
she hasn't been at school the last few days. Make
sure nothing's—you know—wrong.'

'How very kind!' Frances sounded genuinely
touched. 'I wish all teachers took so much trouble!'

'Well, I'm sure they do. I mean, Rebecca is a
special case, in a way.' Marion felt uncomfortable,
but she was hardly sure why.

'I still say it's nice to come across such personal
interest,' Frances insisted. 'There's nothing to worry
about at all, Miss Thomas. Last Tuesday night she
came out in a rash, and swollen glands, and a slight
fever. Most probably German measles. It's been
around. She didn't really feel very ill, and she's much
better now.'

Such a simple explanation—but what bombshell
had Marion secretly feared? This relief now coursing
through her was ludicrous, out of all proportion. 'As
long as that's all. Just that it's half-term next week,
you know, so I wanted to check she was okay before
the break.'

'Half-term?' Rebecca's aunt sounded taken aback.
'Good grief, so it is! No school all week, eh?' She
chuckled. 'I bet you and your colleagues look forward
to it, even if it's not every mother's idea of fun. And
you deserve it, too,' she added generously.

'I quite enjoy the rest, yes.' But Marion's voice
lacked conviction.

'I bet! And I bet you need it, from what I hear of your dedication.'

'I only do my job.' Marion felt faintly embarrassed. What had Frances been hearing, and from whom?

'Huh!' Frances sniffed audibly. 'You sound like my husband. That's what he says when he's been out all hours trying to help some poor parishioner cope with a family crisis. *Just doing my job.*' Even without having met the woman, Marion could picture her expression of fond exasperation. Before she could comment, Frances was pressing on—clearly a born communicator, a sociable being. With this much affectionate warmth in the background, surely Rebecca shouldn't have too much trouble settling down? No wonder Nicol had considered it appropriate to leave the child in this woman's care.

'I tell you what, Miss Thomas,' Frances enthused. 'If you're planning to be around over half-term, why don't you drop round and see Becky? She'd be absolutely made up to see you, and we'd love to meet you, Den and I, after all we've heard.'

'Well, I don't know . . .'

Frances misinterpreted Marion's hesitation. 'She's not infectious any more. It's only a mild one, you know, German measles.'

'Oh, I'm not worried about that.' Marion chuckled. 'I had all the childhood diseases years ago, and I must have been exposed to them again a dozen times since. No, that's no problem. Actually, it's a good thing for Rebecca if she's getting that particular one over with, isn't it?' she added, as the thought struck her.

'Quite. I mean, I know they inoculate against it nowadays, but I still think it's just as well for girls to get it when they're young.'

'I know what you mean. Double insurance.' They

might have been old friends, the way they chatted fluently.

'So you've got no excuse not to call, just for an hour or so—a cup of tea, perhaps—unless you're going away?' Frances seemed unduly keen on the idea.

'I'm not going anywhere.' To be honest, Marion had always disliked half-terms. An unnatural break, this single week, spoiling the rhythm of school life. Too short to relax, too long not to lose the thread.

'Well then! Go on. It would please Becky so much.' There was no doubt about it, Frances was positively longing to meet her. To Marion's sensitive ear, listening between the lines, there was a distinct note of profound curiosity.

And Marion wasn't without a certain interest herself. 'All right then, Mrs Jarvis. Thanks. What day would suit you?'

'Almost any afternoon. I'm usually around because the boys have their rest. It would be a good time for Becky too; she gets bored then, now she's feeling better. And with any luck, my husband will be in for his tea.'

'Shall we say Tuesday, then?'

'Fine. Come about three.'

'I'll do that,' said Marion, while her mind shouted the crucial, unaskable question: *and what about your brother-in-law? Will he be there?*

'And you never know . . .' Frances sounded abstracted, as if her attention had been caught by something else, 'Nicol might even be around.' Had the woman been tuning in to Marion's thoughts? 'He's definitely not flying off again till the end of the week, at the earliest. He tends to spend his days at the British Library and other erudite haunts, conducting his researches, but at the moment he likes to come back to be with Becky when he can.'

'I'll be coming to see Rebecca.' Marion heard her own words emerging far too sharp and starchy, and modified them at once. 'And to meet you, of course.'

'I gather you've already had a fruitful discussion with Nic. That was good of you, Miss Thomas. He was grateful. Now, you must excuse me, the baby's fussing and young Jamie's suspiciously quiet. I left him and Becky watching *Play School*, but he never sits still this long.'

'Of course, Mrs Jarvis. I never intended to keep you all this time. Please tell Rebecca I'm glad she's better, and I'll see her on Tuesday.'

'Right. You know where we live? Past St Peter's, down Church Road, next on the right; then it's the dilapidated house on the corner. They're supposed to be building us a new vicarage, but you know how it is, funds are low, what with the church roof, the organ pipes, the . . .'

'I know how it is.' Marion was smiling. 'And don't worry, I'm very good at finding my way around.'

'Tuesday at three, then. Oh, and Miss Thomas?' Frances had still got a postscript, baby or no baby.

'Yes, Mrs Jarvis?'

'It was kind of you to ring, it really was. I appreciate it, and I know Nicol will too, when I tell him.'

'Not at all. I like to keep tabs on my pupils.' Again, Marion was painfully aware of her own primness. *Only doing my job.*

'If you say so,' Frances remarked cryptically. 'Goodbye, then.' The line clicked. Exit Mrs Denham Jarvis: busy, friendly, a little scatty perhaps? Mother to two small boys, aunt to Rebecca, vicar's wife and helpmate, sister-in-law to Nicol. A cast of thousands, all wrapped up in the one versatile female form. A universal figure, whom Marion admired and respected, even without knowing her. And perhaps, at a half-conscious level, envied a bit too.

Her smile was wry as she slowly replaced the receiver. She hadn't needed much persuasion before accepting that impulsive invitation. She generally made a point of not involving herself in her pupils' home lives. But could she help it if Frances Jarvis was so amiable and hospitable?

No, she reproached herself as she walked back to the staff room. There was more to it than that, as she knew perfectly well. She had a very special soft spot for Rebecca, and obviously the feeling was mutual. These things happened occasionally, and where was the harm? She never allowed favouritism to enter the classroom world; never. But outside school there was a whole different world, and why not follow an emotional lead in it for once? She might be bruised, once bitten (where had she heard those expressions, very recently? Oh yes, she and Nicol Jarvis had used them to describe his daughter: how strange!) but that was no reason to guard against real relationships for ever.

Just for a change, she was quite looking forward to half-term. Her flat needed a good clean-up this weekend for a start. She felt energised instead of depressed at the prospect of the week stretching ahead. She didn't stop to analyse why; she collected her things and walked smartly home to get on with it.

Marion rang the bell, then stood back to inspect the house. She wouldn't have described it as dilapidated, exactly, but certainly shabby. Perched at the end of a Victorian terrace, more imposing than its neighbours, with Gothic touches, ornate mouldings, an old-fashioned oak door . . .

Which was now being opened, slowly, creakily, as if the person the other side found it heavy. And there on the threshold stood Rebecca, glowing with shy excitement, her blue eyes eager on Marion's face.

'Hallo, Rebecca. Feeling better?' Marion stayed where she was, hands in the pockets of her loose-cut checked trousers; relaxed, smiling.

'Yes, thank you,' the child muttered. Then she succeeded in smiling back, newly bold on her own territory. 'It seems funny seeing you here, Miss.'

'People always seem funny at first when you see them in the wrong place.' Marion had been thinking much the same, contemplating Rebecca out of the classroom context. For all her involvement in her pupils, this rarely happened, except by accident or on organised school trips. 'Are you going to invite me in?' she prompted, as Rebecca appeared rooted to the spot, perhaps overwhelmed now that the special visitor was really here.

'Sorry.' She stood back to let Marion past into a wide cluttered hallway. 'Aunty Fran's in the kitchen and she said bring you through. The boys are asleep. Jamie wouldn't go down till half past two. I told him you were coming and he got all worked up.'

'Oh dear!' Marion followed Rebecca to the back of the house. 'I bet your aunt was pleased about that!' She was reflecting that she had probably never heard Rebecca put quite so many words together at once. 'This is a nice house. Do you like living here, Rebecca?'

'Oh, yes,' the child replied without hesitation, 'now I'm getting used to it.' She swung round so abruptly that Marion almost collided with her. 'I didn't like it so much at the beginning,' she confessed.

'It was bound to feel strange at first.' Marion was calmly sympathetic. 'But I'm glad you feel better about it now.'

'I do.' Rebecca flashed that translucent little smile, then pushed the kitchen door open.

If the Vicarage was only partly as Marion had envisaged, Frances Jarvis was a complete surprise. It was shameful, the way people allowed stereotypes to influence their expectations, and Marion was as guilty of it as anyone. Frances had sounded so comfortably maternal, Marion had automatically fitted a rounded, soft shape to the voice. This woman who came forward to greet her now, wiping damp hands on a towel, was slender and willowy, with long legs in denim jeans. Her face was fine-boned, expressive, and her chestnut hair luxuriant and caught back in a loose ponytail. But the voice was instantly recognisable, and the friendly smile matched it perfectly, dispelling Marion's misgivings.

'How lovely of you to come, Miss Thomas! We've been so looking forward to it, haven't we, Becky?'

Rebecca nodded, gazing adoringly at Marion but crossing to stand nearer her aunt. 'It was kind of you to ask me, Mrs Jarvis. Super kitchen!' Marion stared admiringly round. 'Lovely and bright.'

'Won't you call me Fran? Everyone does.' Frances was studying Marion's face with candid curiosity, hazel eyes quick on every detail. No doubt she did this with each new acquaintance, but it was highly disconcerting all the same.

'Then I'm Marion.' She half turned to look out of the window, deliberately moving away from the other woman's intent concentration. 'Big garden you've got, haven't you? I expect you play out here a lot, Rebecca?'

'Would you like to see it properly, Miss? There's a tree at the end, with a swing that Uncle Den made. And . . .'

Frances was laughing. '"Miss"! I'm sure Miss

Thomas doesn't want to feel as if she's at school today, Becky. She's on holiday too, you know.'

'That's all right.' They exchanged smiles. 'I'm used to it. My pupils always call me Miss, wherever I see them. In Sainsbury's, on the street . . . teachers get used to it. There's one little boy in the second year whose mother is a teacher at our school, isn't there, Rebecca, and he even calls *her* Miss.'

Rebecca nodded. 'But I expect he calls her Mummy at home.'

'When he remembers. Anyway, you call me whatever you like—Marion here, Miss at school, or Miss all the time, I don't mind.'

'Well, can I show you the garden?' Rebecca was practically jumping up and down. 'We're digging a pond to put fish in, aren't we, Aunty Fran? We started last weekend. Can we go and look at it?'

Marion turned enquiringly to her hostess. It was her job to make such minor decisions at school, but not in someone else's home. 'I don't mind, if Aunty Frances doesn't.'

'Of course I don't. I'll tell you what, though, I've got a much better idea. It's a super day, and Becky's been cooped up here so long, she's dying to stretch her legs. She could do with some fresh air now she's really better. I can't go out while the boys are asleep, but why don't you two go for a walk in the park? Then, when you get back, it'll be teatime and Denham should be home.'

'Oh yes, a walk in the park! Please, Miss!' It was startling, yet quite natural, to find Rebecca's small hand had reached up to clasp hers, all reserve forgotten in her beaming enthusiasm.

Marion glanced at Frances for confirmation, then smiled down into the child's pale radiant face. 'Why not? It's ages since I went to the park, and it's lovely at this time of year. Wrap up warm, though. There's a nip in the air today even though it's so sunny.'

Frances showed them to the door, buttoning Rebecca's coat. 'Be back around four, okay?'

'Fine.' As Rebecca skipped along with her, Marion was processing her own intuitive reactions. A very engaging person, Rebecca's aunt. A pleasantly rambling sort of house, with a cosy atmosphere despite its size. A house that was due, later this afternoon, to contain Rebecca's uncle and her little cousins, but what about her father? No one, least of all Marion, had mentioned Nicol. He might be coming back to tea—and he might not. She tensed with apprehension at the first possibility, but with an undeniable disappointment at the second.

The park was the kind London is justifiably proud of: gently landscaped, with grassy slopes, meandering paths, flowerbeds, trees and bushes; tennis courts, children's playground, a bandstand. Best of all, there was the lake, tranquil with gliding ducks and darting moorhens, weeping willows stooping down to it, and an island in the middle, thick with foliage and looming mysterious and inaccessible, a fantasy in the midst of this city reality.

Autumn sunlight fell richly gold on yellowing leaves and neat damp turf. It was a delightful feeling, walking among all this, chatting easily to her young companion. Rebecca had loosened up so much, it was incredible. She clutched Marion's hand as she trotted along, offering opinions and observations as if she had been sharing them with her all her life. That insecure shell had been hard, but thin. Her father's return, plus Marion's conscious efforts, had been enough to crack it, and now she was emerging fast. The start of a success story at least, but it remained to be seen how things would work out when the central figure in her life abandoned her again. Which he was scheduled to do any minute, not for too long this time, but how would a second desertion affect Rebecca in her fragile state?

Marion switched her attention to the girl's prattlings. Released from the confines of school she was full of questions and comments, a strikingly bright child.

'Why do shadows get longer and shorter?' she wanted to know.

'It's to do with the time of the day and the year. It all depends on where the sun is in the sky.'

'Is that why they go to one side sometimes and in a straight line other times?'

'That's right. If the sun was directly above us, in a hot country, near the Equator, our shadows would nearly disappear, especially at noon. You know when noon is?'

'Twelve o'clock, when we have lunch. That's why we say afternoon.'

'It certainly is.' Rebecca was nothing if not well-informed.

'My daddy told me that. He's been in places where the sun's right over your head at noon, and everyone goes to sleep because it's too hot to stay outside.'

'I'm sure he has.'

'But if we say afternoon, why don't we say before-noon?'

Marion laughed. 'That's a clever idea. Actually people used to say "forenoon", but now we say morning instead. I can't really tell you why, Rebecca. Sometimes words stop being used for some reason.'

'Oh.' Rebecca stood still, reached out both arms

and considered her own shadow with scientific
interest. 'It's funny how shadows don't seem to be
there when you touch them, but they are really. I
mean, if I stand on your shadow you can't feel it,
but . . .'

They had wandered to the edge of the lake and
now gazed out together at the dappled water. 'How
do you mean, Becky?' Marion was intrigued.

'Well, my father told me about these people . . .'
Rebecca faltered.

'What people?' Marion was even more intrigued.

'In that place where they dropped a horrible big
bomb, in the war. Lots and lots of people were
killed because it made such a huge explosion
and . . .' Rebecca was looking up at Marion for
encouragement.

'You mean Hiroshima?' Marion hid her surprise.
'In Japan?'

'That was it. Well, Daddy said there were some
poor people who were so near the hottest part
when the bomb dropped that nothing was left of
them except their shadows on the ground. Or on
walls, printed where they were standing. You can
still see them now, I think.' Rebecca's hands were
thrust into the pockets of her anorak, and she
stared out at the island as if for inspiration.

'I've heard that, yes.' Marion's glance fell sidelong,
to the top of the fair curly head. 'Your daddy told
you about that, did he?' It seemed strange, telling
such a tale to a small child, even such a bright one.
Not what every parent might have done, laying
such a burden on her imagination, but then he was
not just any parent.

Before Rebecca could reply, a much deeper voice
did it for her. Not a yard away, behind them, and
they had not heard his approaching footfall on the
soft ground, half a minute earlier.

'You disapprove, Miss Thomas? Marion?' They jumped round and apart as Nicol stepped between them. Cool, but grinning at the astonishment in both their faces.

'Daddy!' Rebecca flung herself into his arms, incandescent. 'How did you know we were here?'

'How do you think? Aunty Fran sent me after you when I got home.' He hugged his daughter, still smiling at Marion over her head. 'Good of you to come and see Becky, Marion. We appreciate it.'

Marion won the struggle to stay composed, returning his smile. 'I was sorry to hear she was ill, and Frances suggested . . .'

'I know,' he cut in. 'Typical Fran. Everyone's welfare at heart.'

'Daddy, we were going for a walk.' A jubilant Rebecca detached herself from her father's arms and stood back to gaze up at him. 'And I was just telling Miss Thomas about those shadows of those dead people you told me about, in Japan.'

'Hiroshima. So I gathered. And I asked Miss Thomas if she thought it was wrong of me to tell you things like that.'

By unspoken consent they were moving on round the lake. Nicol laid an arm across his daughter's bony shoulders; his other elbow touched Marion's as she strolled in step, hands firmly in pockets now.

She kept her response well concealed. 'Not at all, Nicol. I think Rebecca can take all that and more, even if some couldn't.'

He smiled again. 'Shall I tell you another thing about when they dropped that bomb, Becky? Something I read only recently?'

'Tell me. Is it very nasty, or interesting like the shadows?' The small face, upturned, registered total trust. Marion's heart stirred to see them, father and child communicating so deeply.

'Not at all nasty, in fact the opposite. That's why I think it's a very important story.' His gaze rested on Marion's, that unique blend of humour and gravity. 'Maybe Miss Thomas knows it already?'

'I can't say, until you tell us,' she pointed out stiffly.

'Right. They had built the city, the walls of the houses, from clay which they brought down from the hills. In that clay were buried lots of tiny seeds, but no one knew that because of course normally they'd just have stayed there for ever, baked into the bricks. But when the bomb fell, the heat was so intense, it blasted all those seeds into life like a huge sun suddenly bursting on them, and they all grew and blossomed, so that within days—or even hours, I'm not sure—the ruins of that flattened city were covered in beautiful blue flowers. Isn't that amazing?'

'Is that true, Daddy?' Rebecca was enraptured.

'According to an eye-witness account I read the other day.'

Marion was silent, her mind working overtime, struck by the profound symbolism of the image.

'Amazing,' she echoed at last, half to herself.

'I like that story!' Rebecca swung her father's hand as they walked side by side. 'We ought to tell it to the others at school, Miss.'

'We'll think about it. Perhaps you'd like to tell them yourself.'

'Would they like it, do you think?' Rebecca was suddenly doubtful.

'I think so, if you told them.'

Nicol was listening to all this, and now he smiled at Rebecca. 'Ill, isn't she?' he remarked to Marion, indicating her pink cheeks and bright eyes.

'I *was* ill. I'm only just better,' Rebecca admonished.

'Of course you are. And it was kind of Miss Thomas to check up on you. And to come and visit you. Us,' he amended, still smiling.

Marion felt defensive. 'It was kind of your sister-in-law to ask me.'

'Aunty Fran says we have to be home by four.' Rebecca consulted her Roland Rat Superstar digital watch, with the air of someone who sensed a tension but could not explain it. 'It's quarter to now.'

'Quite right, chicken. That's one reason she sent me to find you. The boys are awake, and Uncle Den's home. We are summoned to tea.'

'You're staying to tea, aren't you, Miss?' Deserting her father, Rebecca ran round to grab Marion's hand instead.

'If I'm invited.'

'You are—Aunty Fran said so.'

'Of course you'll stay. It's all arranged.' Nicol was conclusive. These Jarvises were a force to be reckoned with.

Marion nodded meekly. 'I shall be delighted,' she told Rebecca.

They stood to catch a last glimpse of the lake. There was no wind, and its glassy surface showed scarcely a ripple. Their three reflections appeared strangely undistorted, yet two-dimensional, beneath them.

Rebecca was thoughtful again. 'Reflections are funny too. Like shadows, but not like them. Even more like the real person, only different—sort of flat.'

'Like what you see in a mirror?' Marion suggested.

'Flatter than in a mirror. You can tell who the person is, but with a shadow you can't. They still don't really look like them, but they make you think of them.' Rebecca seemed desperate to express something.

Marion was caught up in the childish logic, always so insistent, this urge to get at the truth and learn more—one of the elements she loved in her work. 'Sometimes real things remind you of each other but they aren't like them at all. Things, places, people . . .'

'Especially people.' Nicol nodded his agreement, but the glance he shared was with his daughter, not Marion, and she was acutely aware again of their close bond—not deliberately excluding her, but strengthened by mutual grief and healing into a deeper link even than the usual one between parent and child.

Leaving the lake, they headed back along the path to the road. Nicol lifted his gaze to the trees as Rebecca's outdoor shoes clomped through a mat of crunchy brown leaves.

'The leaves are falling off,' she complained. 'I didn't want the summer to finish.'

'Everything has to end, my sweet.' Nicol's tone was gentle.

'Every leaf must fall,' Marion quoted wisely. Then she added, 'If autumn doesn't come, we'll never reach Christmas.'

Rebecca brightened at once, as Marion knew she would. 'That's true!' Suddenly she clutched Nicol's arm, and her voice was shrill. 'You're coming back for Christmas, aren't you, Daddy?'

'I promise, petal.' He stopped walking to lay both hands on her shoulders, confronting her solemnly, his expression so tender, so intent, Marion's throat constricted and she turned away as if caught intruding on a private scene.

'I don't want the leaves to fall off because I don't want it to be winter. But I do want them to because I do want it to be Christmas.' Rebecca frowned up into her father's face, bewildered.

'I think, my little philosopher, you've just touched on the human predicament.' Her father dropped his hands, shaking his head in mock pomposity before walking on again.

'Like father, like daughter,' Marion observed mischievously.

'Are you suggesting Rebecca is a chip off the old block?' Nicol arched his eyebrows, and already she recognised the expression at a subconscious level. Satirical outrage; his own version of Rebecca's screen—one of his official public personalities. Then he lapsed into a rather convincing Groucho Marx impersonation. 'Who are you calling an old block?' he demanded tetchily, imaginary moustache twitching.

Marion giggled, but Rebecca decided this crazy adult conversation had gone on too long, even if it was between two of her favourite grown-ups. Really, the stupid things some of them came out with!

'Can we go home?' she pestered, pulling at both their hands. 'I want my tea. I'm hungry!'

CHAPTER FOUR

JAMES Ian Jarvis, aged three, sat on the living room floor, his stubby legs stretched out straight. It was a good place to sit, for a number of reasons. First, his mother was in the armchair behind him so that he could lean against her knees, a cosy supportive feeling. Second, his cousin Becky was only a yard away, busy with that impossible jigsaw of the Changing of the Guard she always doing. He couldn't make head nor tail of it himself, but he was happy watching her nimble fingers slotting those funny-shaped bits together, and sometimes she let him help put one in place.

Third, it was an excellent vantage point for keeping an eye on young Michael, checking that he didn't hog all the limelight with his fair hair and blue eyes, and all those stupid gurglings and chucklings everyone loved so much. Mind you, he was abnormally quiet at this moment, ensconced on their father's lap, surveying the company as closely as James was himself; but you never knew when he would start squealing or crawling about and getting into everything.

Fourth, there was this new lady visitor, the one Becky had made such a fuss about, now chatting and laughing with his parents and uncle Nic like an old friend and not just some teacher or other. From down here James could watch her carefully, trying to work out why they had all got so excited about her. She was nice enough, he supposed—rather pretty, certainly—almost as pretty as his mother, he admitted grudgingly. But plenty of nice ladies came to visit the vicarage and no one usually turned a hair. So what was so specially interesting this time, so that they all talked about her before she arrived, and looked at each other in that peculiar way, making him feel left out? They forgot how much he noticed, just because he was so small . . . he'd have to get Becky to explain it to him later. She was good at explaining things.

He munched another bite of his mother's gooey fudge cake. Nobody minded the icing smeared on his cheeks or the crumbs dropping on the carpet. They were all much too absorbed in what they were saying. Becky was silent, listening to them. Even that noisy nuisance Michael had turned the volume down on his croonings and squawkings.

'You're not a Londoner really, are you, Marion?' Denham Jarvis adjusted his younger son more cosily into the crook of his arm.

Marion returned his smile. It was hard not to grin spontaneously at the Reverend Denham, even without the extra embellishment of the baby. He was rounder, gentler, altogether less abrasive than his brother; yet there was an echo there if you looked for it, a clear likeness in the sharp blue of the eyes behind square spectacles, the light unruly hair, and that quality of inner strength in the features, however softened.

'Well spotted! I was born in Glamorgan. Is it so obvious?'

'I knew you were a Celt as soon as I saw you.' Nicol's words were softly spoken, yet with an odd emphasis.

'I knew you were Welsh when I heard you on the phone. It's my training,' Frances explained, as Marion turned to her in surprise. 'I studied linguistics. Anyway, telephones always exaggerate accents.'

'True.' Marion sipped her tea. 'But I must say, I

thought I'd lost mine. It's years since I lived anywhere near Wales.'

'Do your people still live there?' Denham polished off the last egg sandwich, steering it expertly away from Michael's clutches.

'No, I grew up in Shropshire. My parents are still there.'

'Very nice too. I love that part of the world. I wish Den would find himself a quiet village church up there, but no chance.' Frances grimaced at her husband, but without rancour.

'I'm a confirmed Metropolitan, you know that. Man and boy. One of us has to be.' Den glared at his brother. 'One globe-trotter per tribe is surely enough.'

Marion found her gaze drawn after his, to rest on Nicol. There was a magnetic quality about his face, so that she wanted to be continually watching it. Alone with him, the effect was alarming and elating at once; but surrounded by the rest of his family, she felt strangely uninhibited. They were so easy to talk to, so comfortable to fit in with. As if she'd known them years, not just hours.

'Don't you mind being always on the move, Nicol? Never putting down roots?' It was a very personal question: would he resent it?

'Roots?' His frown was sardonic, rather than offended. 'What are roots, in this day and age? The age of movement? I'm a citizen of the world, Miss Thomas,' he declared, relishing the cliché.

'Cosmopolitan, not Metropolitan.' Frances reached out a hand to tousle her elder son's hair, as dark as her own.

Marion tutted. 'You'll be telling me next you were educated at the great University of Life.'

'Oh, I was, I was.' From across the room Nicol's smile reached her: direct, quizzical. He leaned back in his armchair, stretching out lean legs in black jeans, crossing his feet at the ankles, linking his hands behind his head: casual, alert. She looked away.

'As a postgraduate, maybe,' Den was remarking drily. 'You honoured Cambridge and Harvard with your presence first.'

'When do you go off on your travels again?'

They were Marion's own abrupt words, but she heard them with a twinge of shock, as if they were someone else's. Immediately, she wished she could take them back. Nicol's brow darkened, and Rebecca's eyes turned sharply up to stare at Marion and then at her father, her small face suddenly pale and pinched.

'At the weekend, probably. But not for long.' He was equable—dangerously calm, but the spark of warning flashed beneath.

Reddening with remorse, Marion looked down into her teacup. Damn her own quick tongue, why hadn't she remembered how touchy, how upset Rebecca would be on this subject? Why hadn't she been more tactful?

But it was the child herself who broke the moment of tension. 'He's coming back for Christmas,' she pronounced staunchly.

'That's right, darling.' Frances smiled down at her niece.

'I think this character could do with changing.' Den held the baby at arm's length, wrinkling his nose in mock distaste. 'He's distinctly soggy in the nether regions. No, it's my turn, Fran,' he added, as his wife moved to get up. 'I'm on nappy duty today.'

But Frances was on her feet. 'Time I was running their bath anyway. Must be six o'clock.'

'*Not* bath!' An indignant James scrambled up, galvanised into protest. Why should *he* have to have a bath, just because Michael was all wet and smelly? *He* wasn't only seven months old!

'You can't go around all covered in chocolate, Jamie.' Rebecca carefully put away the tray containing her half-made puzzle on a high shelf, out of reach of tiny prying fingers. 'You'll get it on everything. Come on, I'll read you a story afterwards.'

'Story.' Beaming now, he offered his cousin an extremely grubby hand, now only too pleased to lead her away. 'Becky story.'

At the door, Rebecca turned. 'Will you come up and see us before you go, Miss? You could listen to the story if you like. I might read *The House At Pooh Corner*. We've got to the one about Tigger coming. Jamie loves them, especially Eeyore.'

'Eeyore,' echoed James, in delighted agreement.

Marion was touched and inspired by this olive branch, this signal that all was well. She smiled warmly, admiring the girl's spirit. 'I'd love to. Thank you.'

'Becky, you're an angel! I'll be up in a minute.' Frances was genuinely grateful. As the two children trotted off, she crossed the room to take her damp infant from his father, grasping the squirming bundle round the middle so that he dangled unceremoniously from her hip. 'She's wonderful with Jamie. I can't think what we ever did without her.'

'I don't know what *'we'd* have done without *you*.' Nicol widened his smile to include Denham, who now stood close to his wife, hands in pockets, acute gaze thoughtful on Marion.

Marion felt even more uncomfortable as she recalled her own initial judgment of this situation, now unfolding itself before her. It had been hasty and inaccurate, and now she felt ashamed—and intrusive.

She cleared her throat. 'Time I was thinking about going. When I've paid my call on the nursery department, of course. I've had a lovely afternoon, but I—I've got things to do.'

'Just let me strip this creature down and plonk him in Jamie's bath, then I'll come and see you off properly.' Frances was already on her way out, firmly clutching her wriggling son.

Marion stood up to call after her. 'No rush.'

'You'll have to excuse me, too.' Den glanced at his watch. 'I've got a parish meeting at seven-thirty and I haven't prepared any notes.' He laid a hand briefly on Marion's shoulder, smiling into her face. She had hardly any need to look up, in order to return the smile. Nicol must be at least three inches taller than his younger brother.

'We're so pleased to have met you. Please come again, and keep up the good work with Becky. We'll be in touch about her. I don't think Nic needs to worry; she's in capable hands.'

'I know that.' From the sidelines, Nicol watched the two of them intently. 'I wouldn't leave her, otherwise.'

'You wouldn't leave her at all, if it wasn't vital to you.' Den's tone was rich with fraternal solidarity. 'We understand that—don't we, Marion?'

'Of course.' Her agreement was vehement and instant.

'See you again, then, I'm sure. Goodbye now.' With a quick wave and another smile, he was gone, into his study across the hall.

In an intimate, enveloping silence, Marion and Nicol confronted each other. It was the kind of hush created only by a sudden stillness in a room recently vibrating with sound and bustle.

Nicol was the first to break it. 'I'll run you home.'

'No need,' she snapped; then, regretting her own defence mechanism, she added, 'I'd enjoy the walk, and it's not far.'

'As you like.' He moved over to the French windows, staring out.

With his back safely towards her, Marion allowed her gaze to linger on him. This two-way pull was in action; that was undeniable. But there was this other dimension too, which she did not recognise. Not just a simple attraction; some more complex element, mysterious . . .

Catching her out, he swung round. 'Do these "things" you have to do include eating?'

'Eating?' She went on staring at him, her face blank.

'Presumably you have to eat. I know you're not afraid of food.' He grinned, leaning on the window frame. 'I've watched you in action, remember?'

'Well, I don't know . . . why?' Marion played for time.

'How about a spot of dinner with me tonight?'

'After all that tea?' she hedged, her mind whirring.

'You hardly ate a thing. I noticed.'

'Oh.' She dithered, then she gathered her composure and smiled at him. 'I might well get hungry again later.' But she hadn't finished prevaricating yet. 'What about Rebecca? Don't you want to spend as much time as possible with her?'

'Naturally, I wouldn't go out until she was tucked up and asleep. Equally naturally, I would check it out with Aunty Fran first.' He was elaborately patient, half smiling, thumbs hooked into his belt. Then he walked towards her, his expression becoming serious. 'Before I go off again, Marion, there's another matter . . . something else I must clear with you . . .'

He came to a halt, so close that the impact was powerful. His voice was strained, his mouth tense, as if he struggled with himself.

'Something else about Rebecca?' Marion stood her ground, intrigued as well as enthralled.

'In a manner of speaking.' He hunched his shoulders, staring down into her face, as if willing her to accept his invitation. 'It's important, or I wouldn't ask.'

'Does it have to be tonight?'

'The sooner the better.' Was it her imagination, or was that a grim narrowing of the eyes, a tightening of the lips?

'Right then. Pick me up at eight, okay?'

He relaxed, taking a step back. Marion relaxed too, but then he reached out a hand to clasp her wrist, and she stiffened again. 'I knew you wouldn't let me down. Thanks, Marion.'

'It's not exactly a sacrifice, being asked out to dinner.' She was on the defensive again.

He released her and stepped back further, but this time he was chuckling. 'I like a woman who knows how to mix pleasure with business.' With this cryptic comment he retreated behind a chair, leaning both arms on its patterned back. The inner battle was evidently over, for the time being. 'Do you like Indian restaurants?'

'Very much.'

'I guessed you would. Tonight I'll introduce you to the best one in London.'

'I expect I know it. I've been to them all around here,' she said airily.

'You won't know it.' He was supremely confident. It was hard to decide whether to be outraged, or excited. 'It's not around here, for a start. It's small and obscure. But I've know it for years, and they do the most authentic tandoori this side of Bangladesh.'

'I'll look forward to it.' She opted for humble acceptance, with a glint in her eyes. No point in arguing with his wide experience, this sense of ancient knowledge which he carried about like a second skin. She didn't even resent it, as she might have done in other men. She responded to it at a deep level; found it fascinating.

Light footsteps approached from the top of the stairs. 'Here comes Becky, to summon you to the ritual bedtime scene. She reads well, doesn't she?'

Now he was the proud parent, tender, expectant. 'Very well,' Marion assured him, confident in her turn on her own territory. 'Her reading age is easily nine or ten.'

Nicol the father smiled briefly at Marion the teacher. 'I've been reading to her since she was a tiny thing in a cot.'

'That's what does it.' Marion returned the smile.

'Oh, Marion, I nearly forgot . . .'

'Yes, Nicol?' The footsteps clattered on the tiles of the hall.

'I don't know where you live. I'd feel pretty stupid, setting out to escort you and realising I didn't know your address.'

In reply she opened her bag and took out a small pack of gold labels, printed in black. With due ceremony she peeled the protective backing from one, reached boldly over and stuck it on the back of his hand.

When Rebecca came in, they were both laughing. 'What are you doing? What are those?' She ran over to them.

'I've got about a thousand of them. They were a present from my mother. She thinks no one should be without self-adhesive address labels, for just such contingencies as this.'

'A useful kind of mother.' Nicol was solemn, but his eyes gleamed.

'I think they're lovely. Can I have one?' Rebecca was impressed.

'Of course.' Marion handed her one, intact. 'There.'

Rebecca gazed at it, her eyes dreamy. 'I'll stick it in my special book.' She sighed, transferring her gaze to her father, then to Marion. Then she became businesslike. 'Now, you've got to come and see Jamie. He's being Very Difficult. He wants his story and he won't let me start without you. Both of you, if that's all right.' She took Nicol's hand and pulled him towards the door, looking appealingly over her shoulder at Marion. 'Please?'

'I promised, didn't I?' Marion was close behind.

'We're on our way.' Nicol strode to the stairs, hand in hand with his daughter.

Marion preferred the mature to the modern, so when she had taken this job she had chosen a flat in a converted Victorian terraced house. It occupied the middle of three storeys, neat and compact. She was content there, but although she owned the lease, it never really felt like home. It was somewhere to live, a background to the realities of her life, rather than the heart of it.

Her lounge window faced the front, and she heard Nicol's hired car pull up outside prompt on the dot of eight. A glance down to the street confirmed that it was a smart red saloon and that he was already standing beside it, looking up at the house. By the time she had grabbed her coat and bag, slammed her door and run downstairs, he was at the main entrance and ringing her bell.

Controlled warmth in his expression ripened to approval as he registered the pretty dove-grey jersey dress, waisted and button-through, simple and suited to her trim soft figure; the freshness of unpainted skin; the bright clarity of dark eyes; the way she had fastened her midnight hair back from its side parting with an old tortoiseshell comb—fashionable, practical, becoming.

He was as informal as ever in navy fitted slacks and pale blue woven cotton shirt, jacket slung carelessly over one shoulder. She smiled a greeting, since words

seemed superfluous. Walking ahead to the car, she
made automatically for the passenger side and waited.
A touch of mischief in his eyes, he opened the
opposite door and held it invitingly wide, ushering
her in with a flourish.

Puzzled, she peered through the car window, and
immediately felt foolish. She was waiting patiently on
the wrong side, the side with the steering wheel. It
was a left-hand-drive vehicle. Her smile was slightly
rueful this time as she walked round to where he
stood.

'Trust you to be different,' she accused, settling
herself in.

He started the engine. 'It's not just perversity. I
have my reasons for most things.'

'You've got used to it, in all the places you go to
where they drive on the right?'

He pulled smartly away from the kerb into a gap in
the passing traffic. 'Try again, Miss. Come on, you
can do better than that.'

Why did he make her feel so alive, with just the
right degree of challenge? She watched him smoothly
changing gear with his right hand, leaving his left to
guide the wheel. It looked quite strange, the wrong
way round. 'Of course! It suits you, because of being
left-handed!'

'Ten out of ten.'

'Well, it's peculiar sitting this side. I feel I ought to
be doing something useful, stuck out here in the
middle of the road.'

'You are doing something useful.' He smiled round
at her. 'You're being an excellent, calm passenger: a
great gift, believe me. I can always tell when I'm
driving another driver: they make much worse
passengers. Get them out of the business seat, and
they become all twitchy.' He paused at a zebra
crossing. 'Never get round to learning?'

'I never felt the need.'

He braked as a green light changed to amber. 'Don't you find it inconvenient? Not being mobile? Independent woman like you?'

'Not at all. I walk. They're remarkably efficient things, you know, feet.' The retort emerged impulsively, on a sharp note.

'I do know that, yes.'

She glanced at him, but his profile was impassive, attention fixed on the road. 'Anyway, it's easy to get around London by public transport, and if I go anywhere else I take the train or coach.'

'And do you often go anywhere else?'

'No,' she admitted. Not unless I have to, her tone implied.

'Not bitten by wanderlust, like me?'

'Not so far.' She stared out of her window, away from Nicol and his field of gravity. They were heading south and west through busy sodium-lit suburbs, already well into territory unfamiliar to her. He evidently knew his way of old, negotiating every turn and junction with rapid steady confidence. All these one-way streets and roundabouts and obscure signposts: Marion was sure she'd never manage it, especially in the dark, even if she had been able to drive. This city was so vast and unwieldy, and she only knew a few small corners of it . . .

'Nearly there.' His voice cut through her meandering thoughts, the lulling motion, the purr of the engine, and she started.

'Good. I'm hungry.'

His silhouette creased in a grin. 'Thought you might be. Me too. Not a bad basis for sharing a meal, eh?'

The Kathmandu was certainly unpretentious, tucked away in a back street in an area of west London where Marion had never, to her recollection, set

foot. That's what London was like: if you didn't need
to go to a particular part of it, you didn't.

The walls of the restaurant were decorated
predictably in red-and-gold flock paper, and hung
with ethnic scenes—but instead of the more usual
pictures of the Taj Mahal and similar notable
landmarks, there were crumbling temples and breath-
taking snowcapped peaks, mountain and valley vistas,
farmers working in fields.

When the proprietor, Mr Mali, had welcomed Nicol
like a favoured family friend and taken their order,
Marion sat back to gaze round. 'You're right—it's a
bit different from the ones I've been to.'

'Wait till you try the food.'

'Where are these places?' She indicated the
photographs.

'Pakistan . . . Kashmir . . . Nepal. Way up in the
north of the sub-continent. That one with the fields is
Bhutan.'

'Bhutan?' Marion frowned. 'I've never heard of it.'
She was a teacher, and her geographical knowledge
had been found sadly wanting. She felt inadequate.

'Many people haven't. It's a small autonomous
kingdom in the Himalayan foothills. Basic peasant
economy, more or less feudal, unchanged for centuries.
I know it quite well because I wrote my Ph.D. thesis
on the agricultural communities there, so I spent six
months of my life living with one.'

Marion's fascination overcame self-consciousness,
and she leaned on the table, sighing. 'Did you really?
What was it like?'

'Primitive. Beautiful. Peaceful. Depressing.'

'Depressing?' She was alight, eager to hear more.

'Villages miles from the nearest road, let alone any
medical facilities. On foot,' he added, with a quick
grin. Marion bowed her head and smiled too,
acknowledging the mild rebuke. 'Whole tribes deci-

mated by regular outbreaks of dysentery. Nine, ten
children wiped out, sometimes in a single week. I
knew a family with twenty-two, so losing a few was a
positive blessing—not so many mouths to feed.' He
studied Marion's face, his tone terse, unsparing when
it came to such absolute realism.

'How dreadful!' Marion's hand was over her mouth,
eyes wide.

He shrugged then, half smiling to see her so
involved. 'It's a whole different way of living, of
looking at life's problems. Those people are fatalistic
and superstitious, rooted in the land. Seasons, crops,
animals. All that has its appallingly bleak side, yes,
but it has its glorious side too. We weren't so different
here once, you know, even in these enlightened,
civilised parts of the world.' He stressed *civilised* with
a heavy irony. 'As a humanist and an anthropologist
I'm bound to take a long-term, global view. In the
violent Dark Ages, or turbulent medieval times, we
might all have lived much as they do. We might have
suffered, but we might have been a lot happier too.'

It was his turn to lean towards Marion, intensifying
his theme. Mesmerised, she was watching each nuance
in his expressive face, responding to shifting cadences
in his animated voice.

'You mean, without the trappings of today? Urban
pollution and all that?' He nodded. 'But is it still like
that there now?'

'Oh yes. I was there—what, ten years ago, but I
know for a fact that very little has really changed.'

'How incredible, to think of all that going on, a
relatively short distance away! I mean, we could be
there in a few hours, by plane!'

He smiled, nodding again. 'Precisely. The age of
movement, as I said earlier today. The novelist E.M.
Forster called it our 'craze for motion', and he was

writing eighty years ago. It's got even worse since then. I think he must have been a prophet.'

Now Marion was on safer ground. 'I know the passage you mean. I've always admired him, too. He went on to say that one day there might be a civilisation that won't be continually in movement because it will 'rest on the earth'. Is that what you mean?'

'That's exactly what I mean. It's my belief that most of us spend our time dashing aimlessly about because we're searching for contact with the earth, which we've lost.'

'Which we've lost.' Marion echoed his words on a murmur, and they seemed to come from inside herself. Then she grinned cheekily, defusing the very solemn atmosphere. 'Of course, all *your* dashing about doesn't count?'

'I dash about so that I can study the reasons why everyone else dashes about. I'm exempt. I do it because I'm interested, and I think I have some useful things to say on the subject. That's all.'

'I know that.' They paused, contemplating each other as the waiter brought two drinks and set them on the table. Sipping dry shandy, Marion went on, 'Which of Forster's books was that? *Howard's End*, wasn't it?'

'Probably. You're the schoolmistress.' He raised his glass in a salute to her before drinking some lager.

'My pupils are hardly old enough to appreciate the major works of twentieth-century English literature,' she reminded him stiffly.

'Except *Winnie-the-Pooh*.'

'Except that,' she agreed, returning his smile.

Their food arrived and became the focus of attention. Was it Nicol's company which added such relish to every bite, sharpened each new flavour and texture—or perhaps vice versa? Either way, Marion had never tasted such spicy succulent chicken *tikka*, such crisp onion *bhajis*, such melting puffs of *naan* bread, hot from the clay oven.

'You were right, Nicol—this is a special place.'

'You bet I was right! And I knew you'd like it, Marion.'

His air of mild arrogance was only partly assumed. Marion knew that, but even so she could not respond with the kind of indignation she might have expected. On the contrary, it seemed to enhance his other qualities of observation, communication, the self-assurance that comes from experience and knowledge. She had never met anyone quite like him before.

Over curries and rice, then Indian sweets—*jellabi* and rich banana ice cream—he regaled her with further accounts of his travels and studies. Every impression and opinion was based on hard fact, but carried the weight of personal conviction, his unique style of interpretation, so that it was always convincing.

Marion was enthralled, forgetting the time and place, losing touch with every reality but this moment and this mood. She was in the grip of a powerful influence and she knew it—and she didn't care. For once, cautious common sense gave way to other senses, and she entered Nicol's charismatic force, and enjoyed it.

And then, over coffee, somehow he engineered a total reversal, and she found herself depicting her own, very ordinary background, her parents, her sister and brother, her early life. Even her feelings about the teaching, and the children.

After that (but how did it happen? Through what subtle cue and encouragement?) she told him about John Wood. Not by name, nor in much detail, but enough to put him in the picture. She might not be deeply marked by life, as Nicol was, but she had known pleasure and pain, and she wanted to match

him in that at least. Her account was brave and
honest, but she had never spoken these words aloud
before and they emerged faltering and husky.

'What a bastard!' His eyes were kind and grave,
resting on her flushed face. *'My wife doesn't understand
me,'* he mimicked, in cynical mockery. 'Fancy resorting
to that tired old gag. How unimaginative!'

'It takes two, Nicol. I fell for it, don't forget.'

'At least you didn't fall right under. Kept your
head above water.' Nicol was deeply thoughtful,
hands clasped round his coffee cup.

'True. As time goes on, I feel more relieved about
that. I mean, it was bad enough, the way it happened,
but if I'd . . . if he'd . . .' Marion blushed furiously
and sipped her coffee. This was ludicrous: unburdening
all this on to Nicol, when she scarcely knew him; yet
it felt so extraordinarily right. She faced him again. 'I
realise now that he never really meant to leave his
wife. I was a—I'd have been a touch of seasoning,
pepping up a relationship that was becoming dull . . .
I think I was a substitute for reality, to him. A
passing fancy,' she added grimly. 'I'm sure I wasn't
the first, and I'm even more sure I won't have been
the last.' She paused. 'I'm well rid of him,' she
declared fiercely.

'You are, Marion. You're right.' Nicol's gaze
wandered to where a loudspeaker twanged out evening
ragas on a sitar, up in a far corner. His attention was
half turned inwards, yet, she sensed, very much with
her. 'Some people do seem to need that edge of
fantasy, to keep their marriage alive. Instead of
working at it, they think fresh blood will prevent it
growing stale. Wrong, in my opinion. Pathetic really,
but there it is: human nature.'

'Some people's nature. Not all, surely,' Marion
corrected.

But Nicol was swivelling in his chair, in search of a

waiter. 'Can we have our bill, please?' He turned back to Marion. 'Isn't it time we were making tracks? Do you know, we've sat here well over two hours?'

'We haven't!' Her incredulity was genuine. It felt more like twenty minutes, yet at the same time an immeasurable evaporation of hours, days, weeks . . .

Nicol settled the bill, then they were on their way east and north through the constant activity of a city night. In the car it was quiet: an enclosed private universe, comfortable, comforting. There was no need to speak, merely for the sake or sound of words. Marion had never shared a silence so mutual and easy.

When they sat outside her house and he switched off the engine, the stillness swelled, all at once suffocating. Marion unfastened her safety belt and gathered up her bag, clearing her throat as she turned to face him.

'It's been a marvellous evening, Nicol. Thank you for . . .'

'Do you realise something dreadful, Marion?' In the dimness his eyes glinted. Was it the lenses of his glasses? No, he had taken them off, folded them up and put them in his pocket.

'What?' She shifted away as far as possible, unaccountably tense.

'I asked you out in order to discuss something. Quite specific.'

'So you did.' Good grief, she was really slipping, forgetting that!

'And I haven't.'

'You haven't.' She felt exposed, faintly ridiculous, as if it was her fault.

'It's your fault.' She jumped: he was a mind-reader, and here was the proof! 'You shoudn't be such a good listener, such rewarding company.' In the darkness, she blushed. 'I realise I've been holding

forth on a number of gripping topics.' She could
sense his grin, rather than seeing it. 'You're the one
who's supposed to say that line, Miss Thomas.'

'Oh, they were. They were fascinating, Mr Jarvis.'

'So fascinating, I never got round to the one I
intended to raise.' His seat belt clicked, his clothes
rustled as he moved closer. She did not recoil but
held her breath. 'It's not like me to get so
absentminded.' He shook his head, self-deprecating.

'I'm sure it isn't,' she made herself say, with an
artificial lightness. 'Can't you tell me whatever it is
now?' she added helpfully.

'No way. Not here, like this. And I've got to get
back to Den's—I said I wouldn't be late, in case
Becky wakes and asks for me. She does that
sometimes and I like to be there, just at the moment.'

'Of course you do.' Marion was firmer now, though
inwardly she was seesawing frantically between relief
and disappointment. So he wasn't even angling to
come in with her now. Had she expected him to; if
he had suggested it, would she have refused? Even
more to the point, might *she* have suggested it?
The whole situation was conventional and yet
extraordinarily new, like opening out an unpublished
map, throwing another light on to familiar terrain.

'What about tomorrow evening? Are you free
again? I've only got a couple more days and I really
must try and talk to you before I go.'

Marion sifted the proposition through at lightning
speed, and reached an instant decision. 'I'm free.
Come and have supper with me, after Rebecca's in
bed. If Fran doesn't mind. It's only fair—my turn to
entertain you.'

'Can't do that: I promised to take Becky and two
little pals out to a McDonald's. Why don't you come
with us?'

'I don't think so, thanks all the same. Not my

favourite form of nourishment.' Marion smiled to herself, picturing the scene.

'I'm rather partial to a cheeseburger and fries, not to mention the chocolate milk shake.' He chuckled. 'But I can't say I blame you. I'll tell you what—why don't I come round afterwards? Say about nine? I'm sure it'll be okay with Fran, but I'll phone if not.'

'That's fine. I'll be here. We'll have coffee.' With that settled, Marion was brisk. Yes, she was curious to know what it was he had to say that was so important, even though her curiosity had been eclipsed, tonight, by the sheer novelty, the effect of his presence.

She turned to him, more confident now, ready to take her leave—and encountered his hands, reaching up to cup her face, fingers on cheeks, thumbs firm under chin, framing, steadying. Her lips parted on a gasp—shock, recognition, anticipation . . .

His mouth was tender and sweet, an experimental contact, then a gradual pressure, a tasting. There was no threat, and only the most subtle of demands. Marion responded readily and generously, offering her own timeless, wordless statement, lip to lip, tongue to tongue.

It was a long gentle kiss, intensifying in heat but not in depth. As his mouth moved hypnotically on hers, his hands slid slowly down from her face to her neck, lingering on her shoulders, then along her arms until they seized her own hands, grasping them tightly so that their two bodies were joined only by lips and fingers, fusing together into a perfectly flowing electric circuit.

At last, with obvious reluctance, he broke the current, drawing back. Now, as she opened dazed eyes to meet his, liquid in the shadows, she was aware of an awakening within her—a quickening, a linking of sensation and emotion—and she knew that

her inner shape had shifted and would never be the
same again.

'Till tomorrow evening, Marion.' Nicol's voice was
low and hoarse.

'See you then.'

She tore herself away from him, finding her bag
and fumbling for the door handle. It went against
every instinct, leaving him at all; and yet there was a
self-preservation about it, a backing-out while the
going was good.

Then she was on the pavement, waving, and he
was revving up the car far more than strictly necessary,
as if he had some extra steam to let out through its
exhaust system, so that smoke and fumes poured out
into the cool night air.

Pollution! She smiled and waved again as he drove
off, fast and rather erratically, along the dark street.
She wasn't sure, but she thought she saw him waving
back as he reached the corner into the main road.

CHAPTER FIVE

AT LUNCHTIME next day, wearing jeans and a T-shirt, her hair tied back in a scarf, Marion sat in her kitchen enjoying a well-earned rest, a snack and a cup of tea. Her floors were freshly vacuumed, her furniture dusted (in some cases even polished), the insides of her windows sparkled. She felt pleasantly tired but even more pleasantly satisfied. It was good to sense this surge of new energy, to actually *want* to get on with all these practical chores—the ones that usually left her bored and frustrated. She hadn't felt like this for months. Yes, it was good: hopeful. No point in pondering too hard about the reason, better to let it happen, take it step by step . . .

The telephone's warble cut into her meditations. She carried the teacup into the hall, picked up the receiver and gave her number as she always did.

'Marion Thomas here.'

'Hallo?' The voice at the other end was high and rather hesitant.

'Hallo? Who's speaking?'

'Miss? Is that you?'

Marion smiled and relaxed. 'Yes, this is me. Who's that?' As if she didn't know.

'Rebecca Jarvis, Miss.'

'Hello, Rebecca. This is a nice surprise. What can I do for you?'

'Well, it's just . . .' There was an uncertain pause, then it all came out in a squeaky rush. 'I've got your number on that sticky thing, you know, the one you gave me and I stuck it in my special book, so I thought I might, you know, give you a ring, and Aunty Fran said it was okay if I did.'

'That's lovely.' Marion waited, as Rebecca paused for breath. As the pause grew longer, she ventured, 'Any particular reason?'

'Yes. It's about Daddy.' Marion tensed but allowed the child to continue. 'We're going out this afternoon, and he said he invited you to come but you didn't want to.'

'That's true. You're going to McDonald's, isn't that right?'

'Yes, but first we're going to see a film. At the Gaumont,' Rebecca added importantly.

'Is that so? I didn't hear about that part of the expedition.'

'No, well, we've only just found out it's on. It's called *Close Encounters of the Third Kind*,' she explained, with laborious accuracy. 'Daddy says it's brilliant and he saw it a few years ago. Have you ever seen it, Miss?'

'No,' Marion admitted. 'I don't go to the cinema much. I missed that one.' Which had been a mistake, she recalled, since the vast majority of her class at the time had seen it and talked of little else for weeks. She had gathered the general gist, but that wasn't the same as comparing first-hand notes.

Rebecca was obviously reporting this to someone with her, judging by the muffled voices which reached Marion's ear. Picturing the girl with her small hand over the mouthpiece, Marion speculated on who her companion might be.

There was no mystery about that. 'Daddy says you ought to see it and it's a major . . . what was it you said?' Rebecca broke off, her voice receding and then reappearing. '. . . a Major Symbolic Work, and you'd understand why if you saw it.'

'Does he indeed?' Marion sounded prim but she was smiling.

'Yes, he does, and he says you should be ashamed, being an educationalist and not keeping up with your pupils' culture and he'd have thought it was part of the job.' Rebecca was quoting, slowly and carefully.

'He says all that, does he?' Marion bubbled with amusement and an odd excitement, but she kept her tone dry.

'Yes, so why don't you come with us?'

'Well . . . .'

'Oh, go on, Miss!'

If Marion had had any real doubts, the pure hope and enthusiasm in Rebecca's voice would have dispelled them. 'Why not? I'd certainly like to see it.'

'That's great! Great, Miss! Rachel and Dawn will be really pleased too!'

'They're coming as well, are they?'

'Yes. They're my best friends now.' Rebecca adopted such a social, confiding air, woman to woman; Marion was momentarily stunned as she realised the extent of the change in the child. 'It starts at a quarter past two, and we're collecting them at quarter to, so Daddy says we'll . . .'

'Please tell your daddy I'll meet you at the cinema. I'll wait in the lobby, about two o'clock.'

'But we can give you a lift in our car if you . . .'

'No, thanks all the same, Rebecca. I'll make my own way there.'

'Will you come and have tea with us after?'

'I'm not sure; I might.'

'Oh, go on, Miss,' she wheedled. 'We'd all like it if you did. Daddy as well,' she added archly.

'I'll see.' Marion knew she sounded like the archetypal adult, fobbing off a pestering child, but she wasn't ready yet to commit herself to that part of the day's entertainment. There was still the evening to consider. This whole thing might be running away on its own momentum, but there was no need to let it completely overwhelm her.

'Okay. We'll see you there, then.' Rebecca knew better than to push her luck when a grown-up used that expression.

'I'll look forward to it.'

'Oh, and Miss——?'

'Yes, Rebecca?'

'Daddy says it's his treat, and you're not to argue.'

'We'll see about that, too. Goodbye now. Thank you for asking me.'

Marion stood for a while, absently drinking the rest of her tepid tea as she stared down at the telephone—that inhuman machine, bearer of such human messages. Then she shook herself into action. Not long to wash and change. She kept the comfortable jeans on, but substituted a yellow cotton blouse for the T-shirt, covering it with a soft loose-knit sweater patterned in swirls of grey and brown.

At one-forty she was sauntering towards the centre of the suburb, a swing in her step, eyes and cheeks glowing in the crisp autumn air.

As it turned out, she threw herself so wholeheartedly into the spirit of the occasion, it would have been ridiculous not to join the party for tea as well. Today Nicol was brisk but friendly, flicking her the odd warm private glance over the heads of his three prattling charges, but always restrained and circumspect. He was so sweet with the little girls, so dashing and attentive, Marion felt herself caught up in their naïve delight, chuckling with their giggles but sharing their feminine response in her own way, at her own level . . .

Her own level, which was definitely not that of a little girl. Settling herself into her seat in the dark expectant cinema, then half-watching the advertisements, the trailers, the first short documentary movie, she was sharply aware of that current again, effortlessly flowing through the three small figures between them, along the row, as if he had reached out to touch her, physically switching it on. He had not touched her. His presence was sufficient to set it sparking.

She understood exactly what he had meant about the feature film. It was, as Rebecca had so succinctly put it, brilliant. Willingly drawn into the plot, breath bated at some of those stunning special effects, Marion knew just why he had wanted her to see it. The hero's desperate need to escape from the meaningless pressure of his life . . . his ultra-human urge to explore the greater mysteries of the universe . . . she understood that all right, and she relished every minute as sheer entertainment into the bargain.

As for the children, they sat agog through the whole length of it, tearing their eyes from the screen only long enough to pass round a packet of Smarties and munch them solemnly, one by one.

Afterwards, slightly dazed in the brash environment of McDonald's, Marion found herself happily engulfing a burger and fries, apple pie and ice cream, along with her four companions. Conversation was lively, mostly about the film and mostly dominated by the younger element.

'It was good, wasn't it, Daddy?' Rebecca was manifestly proud of her status as hostess and personal friend of the teacher, not to mention her highly presentable father. 'I liked the bit where the space ship came down and played that tune really fast and loud.'

'I liked it when the man made a hill out of his mashed potato.' Dawn tucked into an enormous pile of french fries.

'I liked it when the little boy got taken up in the flying saucer. It was really scary, all those clouds and funny lights.' Rachel was not going to be outdone. 'Which bit did you like best, Mr Jarvis?'

He considered. 'I like the scene where they're climbing the mountain and hiding from the helicopters, and you don't know if they're going to make it to the top in time to see the aliens land,' he decided.

'Which bit did you like, Miss?' Dawn wanted to know.

'I'm not sure. I'll have to think about it and let you know at school on Monday. I though it was all terrific.'

'Did you, Marion?' Nicol's eyes were serious, resting on hers.

'I did,' she assured him. 'It was kind of you to suggest it.'

'We all enjoyed having you there, didn't we, girls?' Gravely, he appealed to his daughter and her new best friends, and they asserted unanimously that it had been brilliant.

When they had dropped Dawn and Rachel home, Marion was easily inveigled into going back to the vicarage and participating in the general bedtime rituals. First she got thoroughly splashed by two shrieking toddlers in their bath. Then she listened to Jamie's story, read once again by Rebecca with full expression and sound effects—this time it was a picture book about a greedy caterpillar. After that came Rebecca's own bath, during which the two of them exchanged earnest opinions on *Close Encounters* and its finer points. (She really was shaping up to be quite comically like her father, Marion reflected as she listened attentively to Rebecca's articulate thoughts and impressions.)

At last she said goodnight to the weary little girl and left her to Nicol's final hugs and stories. Feeling quite exhausted herself, Marion was glad to join Frances and Denham for a drink in their newly peaceful living-room.

'Enjoy the film?' Den sprawled, dog-collar mildly askew, in his favoured shabby armchair, smiling across at her.

'I thought it was great. I enjoyed the whole afternoon.'

'Sorry you got enticed back here for all this.' Fran, tousled but calm, stretched luxuriously, savouring that unique moment of relaxation known only to a mother whose offspring are finally tucked up for the night. 'What chaos! It's supposed to be your holiday—and look at your sleeves, they're still wet!'

I really enjoyed all that too,' Marion stated firmly. 'Your children are lovely. That baby's just gorgeous—so good-natured.'

'Trouble is, he knows it. He plays up to the adults and Jamie gets jealous. Typical second child.' Den was wise and tender, discussing his tiny sons.

'Jamie needn't worry. He's a fantastic child, really clever—you can tell he's taking everything in.' Marion felt at home in this subject, just as she felt at home in this house.

'Inherited his mother's brains as well as her beauty.' Den beamed at his wife with affectionate mischief.

'You might say the same about your side of the family, with Michael.' Frances turned to Marion. 'Don't you think he's a lot like Nic?'

In the face of such a direct question, Marion shrugged and looked down at her hands. 'I suppose

so . . . in colouring. Like Den too, and Rebecca,'
she pointed out cautiously.

'It's all that magnetic charm I was actually
thinking of.' Fran was sardonic. 'He's a Jarvis to
the fingertips, that infant. Knows how to get round
anyone, especially if they're female.'

Was it an amicable warning or simply a characteris-
tic wry comment? Not knowing Frances well enough
to be sure, Marion restricted her reaction to a quick
smile and sip of sherry.

'Anyway,' Den mused, 'they approve of you.
They think you're a good thing.'

'I expect Jamie approves of anyone Rebecca
likes,' Marion said modestly.

'True. He adores his cousin. I don't think we'll
have any problems when it's his turn to follow her
to Burnbrook.'

Marion smiled at her host. 'I look forward to
having him as a customer. Won't be for a while yet,
though.'

'Not as long as you think.' Fran sighed. 'They
grow up so fast. He'll be starting in the nursery
class there next year, you know. It seems only
yesterday that Becky was born.'

'What a thought!' Den and Fran were silent in
mutual contemplation, and Marion shared their
silence, respecting it.

'Well, here's an animated scene.' Nicol loomed in
the doorway, resting on the jamb, brows raised in
gentle satire. 'Such quickfire exchange of views!
Such avid discussion!'

'Shut up, you.' Frances pulled a face at him. 'We
were being profoundly philosophical, if you must
know.'

'Runs in the family.' Breezily, Nicol confronted
Marion. 'Are you ready, then?'

'Ready for what?' Taken unawares, she replaced

her empty glass on the small table with a jerky *clunk*.

'We have a date, remember? Some—unfinished business?'

Was she hallucinating, or did a shaft of nervous apprehension ripple round the room, from Nicol's darkened tone and expression, to show itself briefly but clearly in Fran's and Den's faces?

'You still want to talk to me, then?'

'Of course. Today was today, and it was fun. This evening is this evening. The one does not cancel out the other.'

'Right.' So be it. Marion stood up, got into her jacket and flicked her hair out from under the collar. 'You're sure Rebecca's settled? I wouldn't want . . .'

'Becky's flat out, and happy. It's all fixed, eh, Fran?'

'It's fine, Marion, don't worry.' But the other woman smiled, evidently appreciating Marion's concern for the child. 'See you later, Nic.'

'See you both.' With a wave he turned and strode through the hall. Marion added a smile and a word of thanks, then followed him.

'Good room. Nice proportions.' Nicol stood in the middle of it, gazing round. Having him there, in her flat, felt unreal—dreamlike—but at the same time acutely real. Bringing the place to life, completing it in an astonishing way. 'All very spick and span. You must be a tidy lady.'

'Not really.' Marion hovered in the doorway to the hall. 'As it happens I was in the throes of my grand half-term clean-up when your little treasure phoned this morning.'

'Ah yes.' He grinned. 'My little treasure. Does well on the phone, doesn't she?' He walked over to inspect Marion's shelves of books. 'Interesting selection. I like Thomas Hardy too.'

'Coffee?' She was backing gradually away, for some reason, out of the room. 'Tea? A drink? I don't keep much in, but I could manage . . .'

'Coffee would be fine.' He swung round. 'Relax, Marion.'

But she was already retreating to the kitchen, where she drew in some deep breaths, between boiling the kettle and setting out mugs, milk and sugar, biscuits, all the paraphernalia on her one and only tray; the round metal one with the tasteful floral pattern, a present from Jilly and Brian last Christmas.

When she returned, Nicol had moved on to investigate her music collection. 'We seem to share similar tastes,' he remarked.

Marion put the tray down, then crossed the room to draw the curtains, shutting out the dingy London evening. 'Why don't you put a record on?' She cleared her throat. 'Take your pick.'

He said nothing, but chose one and knelt to place it carefully on the low record deck. Marion was also kneeling, a few feet away, her back to him as she organised the coffee at the low table. 'Milk?'

'Yes, but no sugar.' He was preoccupied, concentrating. There were clicks and whirrs, then the strains of the Bolivian folk group, Rumillajta, rising from a thin woodwind wail to rich tuneful harmony, reaching to the corners of the quiet room.

Marion turned then to smile at him, only to find him smiling at her.

'*City of stone*; my favourite.'

'Mine too. And quite appropriate, I thought.'

'Your recent South American travels, you mean?'

'Something like that, yes.'

'Did you see them, when you were there—instruments like this?'

'I certainly did. I heard this music too, up in the Andes.'

'Pan pipes, bamboo flutes and—what are they called, those funny guitar things—charangos?' All the time they spoke, they watched each other, and it was as if the words emerged unaided, of their own accord, while real communication went on at another level.

'Did you know,' he enquired solemnly, 'that the charango is made from the shell of the armadillo?'

She shivered slightly. 'Poor armadillo!'

'But wouldn't it be worth it, Marion,' he moved a little closer, 'to know you'd be a source of beautiful sounds after you'd gone?'

'I suppose so. If you did know.' She handed him his mug, then picked up hers. They continued to survey one another, two denim-clad figures, sipping coffee and kneeling on Marion's thick-pile beige carpet. Inches apart, but not touching.

It would have been so simple to blame that atmospheric music for what happened next, but when she looked back later, Marion came to understand that it was inevitable. Music can only be a catalyst, a key to unlocking a certain build-up of tension, not a cause in itself.

No, there was too much there, flowing between and around them; too much of that electricity, too much chemistry, too much sympathy and empathy, instinctive involvement, mutual respect . . . how could they prevent it translating itself into that most ancient channel of expression, when senses take over from where words must leave off?

Nicol voiced that thought as he put down his coffee cup, reached over to do the same with hers, then laid both hands on her shoulders, gazing into

her face. 'Too many mind games, Marion.' It was a
husky murmur, yet forceful. 'Not enough true
communication. We're warm-blooded consenting
adults, not talking heads.'

Mammals. Even at such a moment, Marion shared
a brief private joke with her inner self. Then she
nodded, because no other response would have
been honest, and reached out to him in her turn.

Gently she lifted his glasses from his nose; equally
gently she set them on the table. Then, leaning
forward, she placed her hands on either side of his
head, drew it towards her and kissed him lightly on
the eyes—those deep blue eyes, now closed, heavy-
lidded to accept her gesture; then on the lean
cheeks; then on the long mouth.

The signal had dropped, the key turned in its
lock. There was no going back. As their lips met,
tenderness swelled to demand, then to a fierce
hunger. Deeper, longer kisses welded them, mingled
them, until there was no distinction between his
mouth and hers, Nicol's and Marion's, fused on a
flood of sensation.

Then they were lying close together on that
carpet, as the lyrical melody of a traditional Inca
song floated on the fringes of Marion's consciousness,
so that in some subliminal layer of her mind she
responded to it, even as her body knew its own
crescendo of response to the sure touch of his palms
and fingertips on her breasts, coaxing, stroking the
peaks into life; his lips and tongue on them, first
one and then the other, teasing, nuzzling, until she
gasped his name aloud and clutched his head against
her chest, craving more and yet more.

Clothes and inhibitions were discarded together,
though for the first time in her life Marion was
oblivious to the process. She wanted the man no
less violently than he seemed to want her. This was

no moment for coy struggles or doubts, not now,
with him about to take his leave—disappear for
weeks on end . . . there was a bond to be
established, cemented, here and now. Whatever
name you put to it, whatever labels you used, this
was what it crystallised down to: this moment, these
feelings.

His hands, eyes, mouth discovered and devoured
her, and she allowed hers to do the same to him,
relished the sight, the feel, the scent of him, so that
no contact was barred or denied, no curve or
crevice kept secret. Until at last (was it seconds?
minutes? hours?) he was able to hold back the tidal
wave no longer, and he was claiming her; and as
she welcomed him into her with tears and cries, she
knew that his possession of her flesh would be total,
and would bring with it her own total possession—
not of him but of herself.

They moved in unison, slowly at first but soon
faster and with a swelling surge, a desperation, an
agony of pleasure which finally exploded into
fragments of pure ecstasy—flames leaping along
power lines from her centre of being to each exalted
nerve-ending, as he groaned and shuddered deep
within her.

Emptying his passion into her, he had filled her
up—fulfilled her. As she lay with him, close and
still, she understood that it was not just this man,
this alien male creature, she desired; it was the
whole person, this complex organism of ideas and
experiences, emotions, mannerisms. In receiving his
body into hers, she had received the essence of
him—everything she already admired and liked in
him, all the things she would learn about him in
future—and it had all become part of her, and that
was what she wanted.

He shifted now, heavy on her, his skin hot and

damp against hers. Then he levered away so that he
could look into her face. The eyes were deeper,
stronger than ever, but softly clouded too.

'Marion?'

'Mmm?' Her smile was drowsy, but it came from
the heart.

'The record's finished.'

'So it is.' The music had come to an end, goodness
knows how long ago, and she hadn't even noticed
as that enveloping silence had settled around them.
'Want the other side?' she muttered.

'No.' Nicol bent to touch his lips to her forehead,
then stroked back the dishevelled dark hair. 'I'll tell
you what I want.' Then they moved to her mouth.
'Better still, I'll show you.'

But she broke coquettishly free to roll over so
that she lay on her front and the black curtain of
hair fell forward to veil her face. 'What, again?'

'Again, and again. All night.'

'Nicol, that's plain greedy!' Her mock disapproval
did not mask her delight.

'Healthy appetite, no more, no less.' He lifted
the screen of hair and peered under it, seeking her
out, blowing in her ear.

'Disgusting!' She shook her head, then lifted her
face to his.

'You shouldn't be so seductive—Miss.' He turned
her firmly over on to her back again.

But his satirical use of her teacher's title struck a
chord, and she sat bolt upright, all but knocking
him flat. 'What about Becky?'

'What about her? You want her permission?'

'Supposing she wakes and wants you?
Suppose . . .'

'Marion.' He pushed her to the floor again and
pinned her there so that he could command her full
attention. 'I'll be off again soon. You know that,

and so does she. She must get used to me not being
there when she wakes up.' In the midst of such
warmth, such fire, he could still be tough, the
eternal realist. 'Tonight,' he went on, more softly,
'I'm staying here with you. Nothing, not even
Becky, is more important than this.' He was moving
in again, closer. 'I told you we had unfinished
business.'

Unfinished business: the phrase reminded her . . .
there was something . . . a reason he was here,
apart from this . . .

But his lips were delicate, tantalising on hers, his
tongue and fingers rekindling that flame, that current
all over again—she was losing the thread, she was
going under . . .

'Nicol,' she whispered, on the edge of the abyss.

'What is it, my sweet?' Recognising her serious
note, he drew back.

'Be there . . . be back by the time they . . . she
wakes up, won't you?'

He studied her gravely. 'Marion, you are an
amazing woman. At a time like this, all you can
think about is Rebecca and how she's going to feel
when I'm missing in the morning!'

'Not *all* I can think about, Nicol,' she protested
weakly. 'I just . . .'

But he held her very tight as he made his promise.
'I'll be there when she wakes up. I shall creep away
from you at crack of dawn, slink through the grey
guilty streets, put myself to bed and pretend I've
been there all the time.' She heard the laughter in
his voice, then heard it drain away. 'But there are
hours before that, during which I intend to make
love to you, and lie with you, and make love to you
again. Unless you have any objections. The night is
young, Marion. That was only the beginning.'

'No objections.' She lay meekly back in his arms,

but inwardly she churned and burned at his tone and his words. He had a way of obliterating all reason, so that all she desired was what he desired, and hang the consequences. It wasn't like her; but then none of this was, and it hadn't stopped her so far. Next week, back at school, with the man safely out of the country, perhaps she might regain her sense and equilibrium, perhaps, perhaps . . .

He was thought-reading again. 'As a schoolmistress you do a grand job. But you're not at school now.' He was trailing butterfly kisses down her neck. 'And you make an even better mistress,' he added, very low, as the trail progressed along her smooth shoulder.

Then her arms were winding themselves about him again, and she was cleaving to him. *The night is young*: yes, he was right.

CHAPTER SIX

NICOL was as good as his word. He was up and dressed before six, quietly letting himself out into the damp daybreak. Then he drove back to the vicarage, where he let himself in, equally quietly, and padded upstairs to his room, carrying his shoes in one hand.

Marion never felt the gentle lips pressed to her forehead, never heard the light tread or the click of the latch. He left her in a deep abandoned sleep, arms flung above her head like a contented child, hair a dark tangle across her pillows. At some time during that long night they had decamped from her carpet to her bedroom—but she was never entirely clear how or when that had happened, either.

She slept on for another five hours. When she eventually greeted the day, the first thing she did was soak for forty minutes in a scented bath. After that, she cooked and demolished a plateful of bacon, eggs, tomatoes and toast, along with several cups of strong coffee. Then, relaxed and restored, she sat down at her bureau in a corner of the living room, and tried to think straight. This was where she always sat when there was something important to consider; it was a pretty Edwardian piece, in polished walnut wood, and had belonged to her grandmother. In Marion's opinion, it had positive vibrations. She had never known her grandmother, but she reckoned old Emily Thomas must have been a forceful woman.

Today, however, old Emily's help failed her. The more she attempted to marshal her thoughts, the

more they eluded her, submerged in this swirl of
irrepressible elation. No, today was for feelings, not
cold logic. The morning after that kind of night
before was not for cool analysis; it was for this
rare exhilaration, these ripe emotions: this glorious
experience of *knowing* her femaleness and rejoicing
in the power of it.

Dreamily, she allowed her mind to marvel at the
dramatic impact of Nicol Jarvis. A month before, she
had never heard of the man, and now he had marched
into her unsuspecting life and taken it by storm.
Captured her, body and soul. As a result, everything
was new and different: the present transformed, the
future exciting. They fitted together, Marion was
convinced of it.

Of course they needed more time; lots more. While
he was away, there would be only too much of that—
plenty of opportunity for mature reflections. But
today she was happy just to sit here and glow and
purr and . . .

It was the telephone again, picking on these
precious moments of private meditation. Sighing, she
wandered to the hall to answer it, but without haste.

'Marion?'

She recognised the brisk warm tones at once.
'Hallo, Fran.' A strange chill tingled through her.
What could be the matter? Had Nicol failed to arrive
home? There was some problem, or perhaps a tactful
message: it had all been a mistake, he had never
intended . . .

'How are you this morning?'

'Fine, thanks.' Was it a straightforward, polite
enquiry, or did she detect a teasing note somewhere
underneath it?

'Good. I'm phoning to ask whether you're free to
come over later, for a meal. Nic asked me to tell you,
it's . . .'

'I was expecting to hear from him this evening. He said he'd phone when he got back from the Library.' For some reason Marion was tense, interrupting Fran with unusual abruptness.

'That's right. He's got some final ends to tie up, then we're having a sort of high tea so that all the kids can be there, and you're invited by popular demand. A proper family send-off.'

'Send-off?' Marion was torn between gratification and alarm.

'Didn't he say? He has to leave at some unearthly hour of the night to catch his plane from Heathrow, back to Central America.'

'I knew he was going back at the weekend, but . . .' *Another couple of days, I thought we had—just a couple . . .*

'Yes, well, it's Friday. Apparently that suits his contacts the other end. Also we thought it would give Becky a chance to get used to him not being here before school gets under way again.'

'That makes sense.' As Rebecca's teacher, Marion could only approve. But leaving tonight . . . flying off tomorrow!

'So, we hope you can come? Nic knows I'm asking you, and I think he's planning to have a talk with you afterwards, perhaps take you out somewhere private after the festive gathering here.'

No doubt he was. Now that she was forced to pull her head together, Marion recalled something about unfinished business. The business that had been finished—or was it started?—last night had been pressing enough, but other levels of reality weren't going to be ignored. Life had to march on, taking her with it.

'Can you make it?' Fran was puzzled at her long silence. 'I've got a hopeful Becky standing right here beside me, making dreadful pleading faces, so I do hope you can.'

Marion swallowed hard. 'Yes, I can. I'll be glad to come. Thank you all for including me. I'm honoured.'

'We're honoured to have you!' Fran chuckled.

'What time would you like me to arrive?'

'If you come about four, you could spend a bit of time with Becky before Nicol gets back.'

'And can I bring anything? Help with the tea?'

'Heavens, no. Den and I will see to all that. Just bring yourself, Marion, okay?'

'Okay, I'll be along at four. Tell Becky I'm looking forward to seeing her later.'

There was a murmur of voices, then Fran announced, 'She's positively gleeful! She can't wait. Now I must get back to the ghastly brood. See you.' Businesslike as ever, she rang off.

This conversation had successfully pricked the bubble of Marion's euphoria, and by the time she arrived at the vicarage she was feeling distinctly strained. Not all that surprising, she lectured herself as she waited on the doorstep. She was bound to feel tired, for a start, after last night; then there was that inevitable edge of uncertainty at seeing Nicol again in the cold light of day. Almost a kind of embarrassment, despite what they had shared. Maybe even because of what they had shared.

Rebecca let her in, all smiles and chatterings, but she seemed paler than yesterday, her small features noticeably pinched. Of course, her father's imminent departure would account for that. Poor kid, she must be feeling upset, but she was putting a brave face on it as she ushered Marion into the hall.

'Uncle Den is in the kitchen and Aunty Fran is seeing to the boys. They're just getting up from their rest.' Rebecca seemed to hesitate, then reach a decision. Standing on the bottom stair, she confronted

Marion. 'Would you like to come up to my room, Miss? I want to—I wanted you to look at something.'

'I'd love to.' Marion achieved her friendliest smile, in a conscious effort to put them both at ease. It was as if her own tension had transmitted itself to the child, by some osmosis.

Rebecca led the way. As they climbed the stairs, Marion defused the slight awkwardness by asking whether the film had given her any bad dreams.

'Oh no.' Rebecca was breezy. 'It was only a film. When I have bad dreams they're about real things, not films or stories.'

As they reached Rebecca's room, Marion restrained herself from enquiring what sort of real things provoked these nightmares. Instead she sat on the bed, wondering what the girl was so keen to show her.

Rebecca went straight to a shelf set into an alcove above her little desk and chair, and took down a shiny folder, bulging with paper. She brought it over to Marion, settling down beside her.

'This is my Special File.' She opened it. 'I keep all my best drawings and paintings in here. And Daddy's letters and cards when he goes away.'

With genuine enthusiasm, Marion examined the works of art—of a high standard, as she already knew from school. Then, concealing her own personal thrill, she admired Nicol's postcards. Bright pictures, cheerful messages in a bold regular hand, from New York and Washington, Havana and Panama, Bogota and Caracas. He must have covered so many thousands of miles, and now he was off to cover some more.

'And this,' Rebecca stated, in an odd dull tone, 'is my Special Book. We got it in Hong Kong,' she added, more jauntily.

'Ah yes, you told me about that. The one you

stuck my address label in, wasn't in?' Marion glanced sideways at her, alerted.

'That's right.' She opened the album, with its ornate silver and red brocade cover. 'I put things in, like programmes of shows, menus, tickets, things like that. See . . .' she pointed to the most recent collection, 'here's your sticky label, and a ticket from the cinema yesterday. And a mat from McDonald's.' It was touching to see these tangible mementoes of highlights from a child's everyday life, methodically preserved and arranged on these white pages.

'That's lovely, Becky. It's good of you to show me.' Marion had a sense that there was more to come, but she did not press the girl. Whatever she was leading up to, Rebecca must take her own time over it.

'In this first part I've got a few photos.' Rebecca was concentrating on flicking through the pages until she located the place she wanted. An earlier section of the book; an earlier era of her short life. 'Here's me and Daddy when I was a baby.'

Marion was only too willing to feast her eyes on these. Nicol had changed hardly a jot in seven years, beaming broadly as he cuddled his tiny daughter: radiant new father, calm and confident, clad in shorts and shirtsleeves.

'Must have been hot?' Marion had to say something, but her throat was constricting at the sight of those muscular lean legs, even more tanned in this picture than she had seen them, just hours ago, when they had been entwined with her own . . .

'I was born in India. It gets hot there.'

'I know.' Marion frowned, bewildered by this inexplicable new terseness in the normally sweet child.

Rebecca turned another page, and without warning thrust the whole album under Marion's nose, letting go of it so that Marion had to grasp it quickly to prevent it falling.

'These are photos of my mother.' The tone was downright sullen now. Instantly, Marion understood, and not before time. She had been a fool, not to have figured this one out: wasn't she the expert on children? Naturally Rebecca would have got herself into a fair old state, making this major decision to share such private memories with Marion. A significant moment, revealing her mother to this latest adult female in her life; showing courage, and intelligence.

Now all Marion's training, as well as her human instincts, came into full play. There was hostility here, as well as anxiety; but who was Rebecca angry with? Her father? Marion? Herself? Her dead mother, for deserting her?

All these were possible, or even probable, as Marion knew. But there wasn't time just now to delve into the psychology of the thing, fascinating as it was. She must respond generously to Rebecca's gesture, or it might be wasted. Worse, it might cause more pain than release. This was a major step in the girl's emotional development, and it must be handled carefully.

She bent to study the photographs, while Rebecca sat silent beside her, curiously distant, yet watching her closely. First impressions presented family groups: Nicol again with the baby; a smiling young woman with a toddling child, a Cantonese *amah*; the same young woman again, standing on her own, beautifully dressed. Groomed and svelte, even in such tropical conditions, by the sea or in a back garden . . .

A closer look registered details: the fact that the woman was dark, with straight shining black hair cut in a chic layered style to frame her face, brown eyes, olive complexion. Rebecca had certainly inherited her father's colouring rather than her mother's. She resembled him far more altogether, in feature and expression . . .

Yet there was such a sense of recognition about this woman in the pictures—the most extraordinary familiarity which grew with every passing second—as if Marion knew her, inside out, better than an old friend. Crazy, of course: Andrea Jarvis had been dead for over two years, and Marion had never met her. But there was something, some element there, strange, profound, a shadow . . . an echo . . .

With a sharp cry, Marion leaped to her feet and the book tumbled from her hands, slipping through suddenly inert fingers to the floor. Rebecca stooped to retrieve it, then stood and faced Marion, clutching it against her chest. The expression in her pale face was a poignant blend of pity, shame, defiance and fear.

'Rebecca!' Marion gasped for breath, let alone words. Her mouth worked, soundlessly, like a fish violently flung to dry land. At last she managed to squeeze the crucial question out. 'I—I—is that your mother?'

Rebecca nodded, still silent, her eyes fixed on Marion's face.

'She—*she looks just like me*!'

Only as the actual sentence formed itself did its true meaning strike home. And the meaning hit Marion in the solar plexus, so that she reeled, grabbing at the headboard for support.

Rebecca nodded again, evidently at a loss for words.

'But . . . why didn't you tell me? I mean, before this? Why?'

Marion sank down on the bed, now weak and shaking. Of all the secrets the child might have had up her sleeve, this was the least expected—and, for reasons not yet quite clear to Marion's jumbled mind, the most devastating.

Rebecca found her voice at last. 'Daddy was going to tell you. He kept saying he was. We all told him he should—Aunty Fran did, and Uncle Den, and me. He kept saying he would but then not doing it. This morning he told me he still hadn't. He told us not to tell you. He wanted to tell you himself, explain about it himself. But . . .' she shrugged, but her tone became firmer and her blue eyes steadier on Marion's, 'I wanted you to know. I wanted to tell you, because he's . . .' she faltered; then suddenly her eyes, nose and mouth crumpled as tears threatened to shatter that precarious poise. 'He's going away tonight and you still didn't know and . . .'

Marion held out her arms and gathered the little girl into them. Her own shock was total, but this basic childish need was more urgent. Rebecca wept profusely against her shoulder for several minutes, while Marion rested her chin on the untidy fair hair, her brown eyes dazed.

When the sobs lessened, Rebecca raised a brave tearstained face. 'I'm sorry, Marion.' It was the first time she had used Marion's name, but neither of them really noticed it. 'I didn't want to do it, if it was wrong, but . . .' she hiccuped. 'But I was afraid Daddy would go away without telling you the truth, and even though Aunty Fran said I *must* leave it to him, I just couldn't wait any more. I'm sorry if it gave you a bad surprise.'

'It's certainly a surprise.' Marion was gently wry. She took both Rebecca's hands in hers, staring into her face. 'Was your mother really so like me? As much as she looks, in these photos?'

Rebecca nodded gravely. 'Yes, she was. Her face was, and her hair, and all that, you know. But she didn't wear the same kind of clothes.'

'No, I can see that,' Marion tried not to sound sarcastic.

'I don't really remember her very well. I think she looked just like you, but not really like you underneath, if you see what I mean.' Rebecca was trying very hard to be helpful, after causing such a disruption, but she was exhausted now and her voice and gaze dropped.

'I know what you mean.' Marion sifted all this through. Rebecca's own words replayed themselves to her—from only two days ago? Could that really be all? So innocent, they had seemed at the time, and now they stood out like beacons in a dark landscape, beaming a message.

Like shadows . . . like the real person only different . . . they don't really look like them, but they make you think of them . . .

And Nicol had glanced at his daughter in agreement, in warning; a clear clue, with the benefit of hindsight, but how could Marion have guessed at anything so unlikely, so outlandish?

The wild shock was already hardening into a frozen resignation, a different kind of wound, bitter, throbbing. She should have guessed, all the same; she should have realised, with her experience of men, that such attachments are rarely what they seem. It was never herself, the real Marion Thomas, Nicol had wanted. All along, there was bound to have been some ulterior motive, some hidden layer: a man like Nicol, an ordinary woman like her . . . she should have worked it out . . .

Marion was a reflection, a fleeting shadow of the late wife whom he had loved; no more and no less. His response, on meeting her (no doubt primed by Rebecca so that he knew what to expect), had been predictable. And then, equally predictably, he could not bring himself to confess, to put her in the picture—not until he had played the game out to its logical, triumphant conclusion. Given full rein to this—what could she call it?—recalled passion. Surrogate emotion. Aimed at someone else, someone dead, not the living, breathing, *feeling* woman in his arms . . .

Marion shuddered. Like making love to a ghost. Her gorge rose; nausea clenched within her. It was sick, sick! Degrading to all concerned! The perpetrators, no less than the victim. Not that she could really blame the child, or anyone else besides Nicol himself. They had all been remarkably circumspect, when you considered it. Nicol had told them to say nothing, and they had obeyed his wishes—until now, when Rebecca could contain herself no longer. She had chosen this dramatic way of enlightening Marion, not through cruelty but simply because it was difficult to muster direct words on such a delicate topic, and no wonder.

As for Den and Fran, they had thrown out discreet hints from the first time she had met them: inspected her with more blatant curiosity than a mere acquaintance might reasonably expect, shown far more interest in her, more warm hospitality, than her position really justified . . . Then there was the way Rebecca had followed her round at school, right from the beginning—cottoned on to her as if she was some kind of a lifeline. Everyone had noticed it, and when she had mentioned it to Nicol, at their first meeting, he had only observed that he wasn't at all surprised. Now she understood that; and the way he had gone on to involve her, woo her—almost like a man in the grip of a compulsion.

Yes, it all slotted together only too well. She hadn't been so fluently accepted here in her own right. She was a reincarnation; a reminder of the Andrea they had lost, not Marion, new friend, new teacher, new lover . . .

Her head swam and her insides churned, but she tottered to her feet, controlling her body and voice for Rebecca's sake. The child had suffered enough. It was not her fault.

'You did right to tell me, Becky. I'd have found out very soon, I'm quite sure.' *When your dear father saw fit to tell me.* 'But listen, I'm not feeling too good. I don't think I can stay for tea after all. Please will you tell Aunty Fran I've changed my mind and I'm feeling rather sick, so I decided to go straight home and not risk . . .' Risk what? Confronting anyone? Exploding, sullying their peaceful home with her bitterness? 'Infecting the children,' she finished lamely.

'It's not because of this? Because of what I've told you?'

Rebecca was so agitated, it was important to soothe her. 'No, no,' Marion lied desperately. 'I wasn't feeling quite myself when I woke up this morning.' Well, that was true enough. 'I think I might be sickening for something.' *Fallen right into it.* 'So, tell them I'm sorry, okay?'

Rebecca was still deeply concerned. 'Maybe it's German measles, Miss. Maybe you caught it from me and now you're . . .'

'No, Becky.' Marion smiled wanly, and reached out to lay a hand on the child's head. 'I've had it. Don't worry, it's not that. It's not your fault,' she stated firmly, hoping the girl would understand that she meant it at all levels.

'Okay, I'll tell them.' Rebecca was defeated now, sheepish, her voice was a tight tiny sound. 'I'm sorry you don't feel well, Miss. I hope you'll be better enough to come to school next week.'

'I'll be there.' Marion was grim. Where else would

she be? What other haven was there, after such a revelation?

'Shall I say goodbye to Daddy for you?' Again that thin, high little tone. Marion turned at the door. The child was sitting on her bed, still clutching the book, the incriminating evidence.

'Yes, do that. Say goodbye to him for me.'

Then she closed the door behind her and walked downstairs, sedately, refusing to hurry; unable to hurry, even if she wanted to. Her legs moved unwillingly; she felt suspended above the floor, outside herself, away from reality. She held the banister rail tight as she went.

From the kitchen came sounds of clattering and humming, with a radio in the background. Den was happily engaged in preparing supper. From the bathroom on the half landing, squeaks and shrill comments indicated that Michael was having his nappy changed, and James was helping.

Silently, Marion let herself out of the house and set her face and feet on fully automatic, heading for the sanctity of home. She forced her chin up, kept her gaze on the world. Wearing inner bruises on the surface was not her style, and no one, not even Nicol Jarvis, was going to change that.

CHAPTER SEVEN

HEAD high, cheeks aflame, Marion marched down
the road, round the corner into the High Street—
past shops, offices, faceless people milling about
their business, perhaps colleagues or pupils and
their parents but (thank goodness) no one she
recognised . . . round more corners and along more
streets, into her own quiet residential area.

She had half hoped, half feared, Fran or Den
would rush after her; summon her back, alerted by
Rebecca, ready to reassure and explain. But nothing
happened, and it was probably just as well. Marion
had no wish to lose her temper with either of them,
and the way she felt, she would have been bound
to. Or worse, their concern might soothe and
mollify, and Marion was all too willing to be
soothed and mollified. But the thin voice of reason
lectured her that she needed to be alone now—let
the full significance of this hurtful discovery sink in,
weigh it up before she allowed herself a public
reaction.

No, it had been a brutal way of finding out, but
really it was fortunate. At least it had left her a
speedy escape. With Nicol there in the flesh—
attractive, articulate—even with Fran and Den
offering words of genuine comfort, her resistance
might easily crumble. And a shock like this was too
complex and profound to be fobbed off with trite
instant excuses. She must give it careful, cool
thought, and time.

Lots of time. Marion's smile was dry. Good thing Nicol was off for a few weeks. As soon as she reached her flat, she'd lock herself in, put the door on the chain, take the telephone off the hook, lie low until he was safely out of the country. Never mind if he came after her, no matter how long or loud he knocked or rang or . . .

She was within sight of home, and traffic had thinned to the occasional passing vehicle. Here was one now, slowing almost to a halt behind her but still throbbing at her heels, oddly menacing. Good grief, not a kerb-crawler! They enraged Marion at the best of times, and at this moment she needed one like a hole in the head. Stupid, insulting oafs, on the prowl for unattached females, with nothing better to do than . . .

She quickened her pace, purposeful. The car followed. Out of the corner of her eye, she registered its shape and colour. Smart saloon. Red.

She swung round, on a reflex; and at the same split second, the driver was flinging open his door, jumping straight out on to the pavement, bare inches from her. Emerging from the wrong side, her mind crazily noted; the passenger side. Of course, it was a left-hand-drive car. Being driven by a left-handed person.

'Marion!'

She confronted him—eyes blazing, mouth clamped tight shut. A severity of tension tightened Nicol's expression and his tone, but no trace of shame or guilt. Marion's nervous rage boiled higher.

'Thank God I reached you, before you went to ground!'

Irony twisted her lips again. How perceptively he read her, even after such a brief acquaintance! But she must remember that to him, she presented no exciting novelty, no mystery package, as he did to her. Just a reconstituted version of someone who had been close to him, very close; who was very familiar indeed. Perhaps the uncanny likeness was accurate through and through, she speculated wildly, not only on the surface.

'Marion?' When she remained grimly wordless, he leaned nearer, acute eyes earnestly searching her dazed ones. He made no attempt to touch her, but his physical proximity was a violent assault on all her senses, sharpened by this seething anger.

'Please, Marion?'

She stared, incredulous as well as infuriated. Please? Please what? What did he mean, *Please*? Her fingers curled into fists, her face showed more anguished conflict than she guessed; and still she kept silent.

'We've got to talk. Surely you can see that.' He waited for a reply, then cut his losses. At least she had not actually turned tail and fled. He pressed that small advantage, knowing a crisis when he met one. 'Please, Marion, get into the car.'

He was so firm, yet so level—even tender—it lulled her into a slight response. She shook her head.

He gathered his considerable control. 'Marion, I'm sorry. I'm sorry you had to find out that way. It was never my intention, but it wasn't Becky's fault, it's entirely mine. I meant to tell you before, and I'm sorry I didn't. I'm sorry about—all of it.'

All of it? Her stare became a glare, and the wry shadow deepened. She was there to bet her bottom dollar he wasn't sorry about *all* of it! Not the outcome, at any rate; not the victory, the satisfaction . . .

But Nicol saw the bitterness which surged through her, and he felt it cut him like a blade. At once he modified his tactics. This woman was in shock, and

he himself had a flight to catch. It was time for
urgent action, not cautious pussyfooting around.

With no warning and in one fluid movement, his
hand snaked out to grab her just above the elbow.
Wiry fingers closed on her arm, and she felt the tips
of them biting into the soft skin through layers of
clothing; then felt her body pulled, dragged towards
his. Then the other hand was on her other arm and
he was gazing deep into her face, the brightness of
his eyes imploring, demanding, a right to be heard.

'Just listen to me, Marion. Rebecca told me what
happened, as soon as I walked in. She feels pretty
terrible, but I couldn't stay and comfort her. I left
her with Fran, and came after you because I knew
how you must be feeling.'

His steady, emphatic words, combined with that
harsh grip, achieved the desired effect. Marion's
tongue was loosened at last. She had not struggled
against this close enforced contact, but now she
flung up every defence, in the form of a scathing
attack.

'You knew how I'd be feeling, did you? How
clever of you! Not just the macho brute force . . .'
she shook her arms, as far as his iron clamps would
allow, 'the amazing insight as well! But then we all
know you're more than a pretty face, don't we,
Nicol?'

He ignored the sneering sarcasm, but recoiled
from the wounded pride behind it. 'I do know how
it must look to you, Marion, but you can't really
expect to understand anything on this evidence.
Rebecca is a child,' he reminded her—so reasonable,
so right, so *infuriating*. 'We're a pair of intelligent
adults. Let me come home with you now, and give
me the chance to put you fully in the picture. I've
been on the point of doing that, right from the
start, don't you see? As soon as I realised . . .'

'My convenient resemblance to your late lamented wife? Oh yes, I'll bet you were! I'll bet!'

She was so cynical; dulled, buttressed with pain. It was like trying to drill through a concrete slab, but Nicol persevered, accepting his responsibility. 'I kept telling you I had to talk to you—didn't I?' His fingers tightened on her arm. 'Didn't I, Marion?'

'Oh, you kept saying it.' She was sceptical now—head tilted defiantly to one side. 'But somehow you never quite got round to it, did you, Nicol? Among all those other . . .' she gulped, and he saw how close she was to tears. 'Not till you'd . . .'

'Till I'd what?' He was gruff now, eyelids heavy.

'Had what you were after!' She was beside herself; almost triumphant in her suffering. 'Got me into bed,' she elaborated, in case he had missed the point.

It was not a busy street, and Nicol was not an inhibited man. But now he glanced round, taking a step back, drawing her after him in the direction of the car. 'I think,' he stated, with quiet deliberation, 'we should go to your place and discuss this thing in private.'

'You'd like that, wouldn't you?' she taunted, pushing herself further all the time, feeling the trap of fury snap on her, ensnaring her. 'You'd enjoy that. You might even engineer a repeat performance—set you up nicely, wouldn't it, before you fly off to exotic parts! Another notch for your belt! Another . . .'

Her distress was overflowing, right into his face. If both her hands had not been efficiently pinioned, she might well have been reduced to slapping it, into the bargain. 'Marion!' he frowned now, a warning.

But she was into her stride, a ranting torrent. 'What was it like, Nic, making love to a—a wraith?

A hollow sham, a pathetic substitute for the real thing? Was it adequate? Disappointing? Did I let Andrea's memory down, or was I a credit to it?'

'*Marion!*' This time he shook her, hard, eyes and voice dark with outrage. 'Don't!'

'What's the matter?' she mocked. 'Not ladylike enough for you? You didn't worry about that last night, did you? Not when you . . .'

'Shut up!' His jaw clenched and jutted; a muscle clearly twitched in his temple. That instinctive gentleness, laced with remorse, had been turned inside out, goaded into a gritty impatience. 'Just shut up, woman.' Keeping a firm grasp on her elbow with one hand, he reached behind him with the other to open the car door. 'Get in,' he ordered, in a tone which meant business.

But Marion seized her opportunity. Jerking away, she retreated a few paces, eyeing him warily the while, a cornered prey. Gaining distance, she recovered a little dignity. Self-respect emerged from where it had been hiding, smothered by shock and angry self-pity. On a more composed note, she tackled him again.

'I won't come with you, Nicol. I've got nothing to say to you, and whatever it is you want to say to me, I don't particularly want to hear it. So please just go away, leave me alone.' She turned her face away then, and her voice weakened, but she stood her ground.

Nicol had no intention of leaving her alone; not yet; not until he was good and ready. His frustration rose, as hers waned: a seesaw of heated emotion. 'You're damn well going to hear me out! If I have to lay siege to your door all night, you'll bloody well listen to me, Marion!'

Suddenly she was bone-weary, deflated. 'You're supposed to be on a plane in a few hours, don't forget.' Her turn to be the voice of reason. 'Nicol, don't you think we both need to put space between us for a while? I need time to think about—all this. I can't cope with any more . . . I just want to . . . I don't know . . .' She shrugged, the words fading into bewildered despair.

The appeal in them—the mute hint at real communication—stopped Nicol in his tracks. His gaze locked with hers, and for endless seconds they transmitted and received indecipherable messages: a bombardment of hope, fear, depression, reproach. A shifting kaleidoscope of feelings; shared and private recollections; human dreams.

Nicol's face worked through a process of decision and conclusion. Then he stepped back, visibly relaxing as he thrust his hands in his pockets. And, unbelievably, smiled.

It was such a transformation—such a softening— no tough strategy could have undermined Marion's stubborn barriers as this did. She felt some of her own stress ebb away, and a tiny ray of hope flow into its place. In an unconscious gesture, she lifted one hand to him.

'Nicol, perhaps if we . . .?'

But the tables were turned; he had taken her point. 'No, you're right—I shouldn't have bullied you. We need time. You'd have found out, one way or another, and now you have and you must deal with it as best you can. I've got work to do. We've both got work to do,' he amended, 'yours no less important than mine. Probably more important than mine,' he went on, reflectively, 'since it involves caring for *my* child.' There was a quirk of humour beneath the serious statement. 'Of course you were upset, finding out that way. It must have been traumatic. Of course you were furious with me. But now you know, and . . .' his gaze intensified on hers, 'I hope you won't let it affect your attitude to Becky. In fact I know you won't. You're far too mature for that, and you understand that she'll need you now, more than ever—after this, and with me away . . .'

'Yes, I know that.' She acknowledged his challenge with a proud resignation. He could rely on that, her professional integrity and strength, to the bitter end—and he knew it.

There was a short pause, then Nicol said softly, 'I'm going to leave you now, since that's what you want. I'm not going to insist any more. But when I get back, we've got to talk it through properly. I want you to understand how it happened. There are things you don't know—things I must explain. When we can be calm, without resentment or—or . . .' he hesitated, 'or passion. Two rational beings.' He stepped towards her; she did not move. 'Will you promise me that?'

Marion nodded, but she was fighting the dawning of a new, bleaker despair. He made it all sound so final. An episode that had flared and then finished. A brief encounter, now ended, so that there were only dissections and post-mortems to look forward to.

'I don't have any regrets, and eventually I hope you won't either.' His voice had dropped low. He reached out to take her hand, lightly, without pressure. The touch fizzed through her, at a depth that steel grip had left cold. 'I realise you're wishing you'd never met me. But what you gave me last night, you gave freely, and beautifully. Thank God you can't take that back now, Marion, whatever happens to us.' Then he added, even lower, but with an unashamed gleam, 'What's more, you'd better believe this, Miss Thomas. I knew exactly who you were, every second of that time. I'm not given to living in the past. You aren't, and you weren't, any kind of substitute—for anything or anyone.' His grin was fleeting, and sardonic. 'Whoever I laid last night, she was no ghost.'

The sheer warmth, the wicked wit, of the man seduced Marion's smile through the clouds. Noting it, he smiled back, lifting her chin with one gentle finger. Then he bent to brush her lips with his: once, twice, sweetly lingering. Tantalising reminders of what had been—and what might have been.

Then he was brisk, decisive, as he climbed into his car and slammed the door, reached for his seat belt, fitted the key in the ignition. A man living in the present, not the past. Or more likely, the future: probably his mind was already ahead of him, halfway round the world.

'Goodbye, Marion,' he called, through the open window. 'Take care of yourself—and Becky.'

'Take care.' She murmured the echo, barely shaken from her strange stupor by the roar of the engine.

But her farewell was drowned by the swish of tyres as he swept the car round in a three-point turn. Then he was just a waving hand, receding down the street. She had been affectionately dismissed.

She turned and walked slowly in the opposite direction. Why did she feel so cheated, so defeated? It could have been worse: at least he had punctured that agonising, blinding anger.

She frowned, shaking her head, depressed. That was just it, of course. Half of all this was due to her own gullibility. He had taken advantage of it— spotted her vulnerable inner self—won her over. He had mounted a successful campaign, based on that remarkable physical resemblance to his wife, to ensure her support for Rebecca. Using blatant deception, he had encouraged her to become involved, not just with the child, but with the whole family; most important, at a deep level, with himself. Now he had even managed to wheedle a sort of forgiveness out of her for the whole thing . . . and then left.

Oh, he was the clever one, no doubt of it! A brilliant manipulator, as so many sensitive men were. In her initial panic, she had fled, evaded him—but he had sought her out and wooed her all over again, using that lethal combination of toughness and charm. Now here she was, in thrall once more, and he was gone, leaving her confused and wrung out, with only a prospect of weeks and weeks of suppressed suspense and disappointment.

Laboriously Marion climbed the stairs to her flat. Everything in it seemed just the same, though it surely had no right to. Her weary glance fell on the bureau in the corner. He'd said one true word: there was plenty of work to be done. She had the weekend to plan the next half-term's lessons, mark all those books she hadn't got round to during this frenetic break from reality.

Or was this a heightened reality? And now she was losing sight of it, bumping back to solid earth? Marion shivered. She would not dwell on that. She would shut herself in here and get on with normal life. As far as she was concerned, Monday couldn't be here soon enough.

'These afternoons are drawing in.' Crunching through a pile of dead leaves, Jilly kicked at them gloomily. 'Another month, and we'll all be going home in the dark. I hate November!'

'I rather like it.' Marion was pensive. 'It fits in with my mood.'

Jilly glanced sideways, as they walked together along the suburban pavement. 'Grey and grim?'

'Oh, come on, I haven't been that bad!' Marion achieved a kind of cheery leer. 'No, just—I don't know—suspended and colourless. Neither one thing nor the other.'

'Suspended between what? Neither what thing nor what other?' Jilly skipped ahead so that she could stop and confront Marion. Her round face was a comic study in avid curiosity. Her friend and colleague had been behaving in an odd way this last week or so; not so much depressed as repressed, even more serious and self-contained than usual. 'What's the matter, Marion? What's happened?'

'Happened?' Marion looked deliberately blank. 'Nothing,' she lied. 'You know me,' she added. 'I tend to get a bit fed up around this time of year— the festive season, and all that. It's just my perversity. Take no notice.'

'Hmm. Yes, I do realise that.' Walking alongside again, Jilly controlled her disbelief, though not without difficulty. Tactfully (or so she thought) she changed the subject. 'Hey, I've been noticing, and I'm not the only one. Your little problem pupil— Rebecca, isn't it—she's a different girl since half-term. All smiles and chat, it's amazing. What have you done to her?'

Marion jumped, very slightly, flicked a quick glance at Jilly, then relaxed and brightened. 'Yes, she's really broken through. She's a great kid. Such spirit.' She paused, to collect herself, making a vain attempt to conceal her personal satisfaction. 'I'm really pleased,' she confessed.

Her smile, and the faint flush that went with it, were not lost on Jilly. 'You must be. Things improved at home, or what?'

'Well, they got better, but . . .'

'After you met the father, you mean?' Jilly was losing the struggle not to sound too intrigued. There was more here than met the eye. Marion was circumspect at the best of times, but now she was being positively cagey. It was irritating when you were as interested in human nature as Jilly was—and genuinely fond of Marion, of course.

'After he came home, yes.' Marion's tone was flat, her gaze straight ahead. 'But he's gone off again now.'

There was a short silence while Jilly hoped to learn more and was disappointed. 'But the child's accepted the situation,' she finally prompted, 'even though he pushed off again so soon?'

'She seems to have done.' *Thank God, after what happened the day he went . . . she could have slipped back to square one, or worse . . .* 'She's a strong character, is Rebecca, and I know now what excellent support she's getting from the uncle and aunt.' No harm in admitting that much. 'I must say, Jilly, I admire her. And it's good to watch her participating in class. I'm delighted.' *And I'm relieved and grateful, and . . .*

'From the little I saw of the papa at that parents' meeting, strength of character is a family tendency.' The topic of the Jarvis father, and how Marion had railed at him, mistaking him for the Jarvis uncle, had aroused much amused speculation in the staff-room, but if Marion had any opinions, she had kept them to herself. Even her notes on the interview had been terse and barely adequate.

'You could say that.' Marion was wry. Strength of character, yes, and subtlety, and a determination to get one's own way, and . . .

'Well, I'm glad it's worked out okay.' Jilly halted and faced Marion, hoisting her duffel bag up under one arm. 'We all know how much you've put into getting the girl to emerge and relax. It's your great gift. Everyone admires you for it.'

'Thanks, Jilly.' *More than you'll ever guess, my friend.*

'This is where I leave you. I'm meeting Brian at his office.'

'Right. See you Monday, then. Have a good weekend.'

'Oh, we generally do. You too, Marion. Anything lined up?'

'I'm going down to my sister's, in Sussex, actually.'

'The one with the two children?'

'That's right. Diana and Joey.' It was quite easy to sound enthusiastic. Marion was looking forward to the change. Her flat was oppressive these days; her own company unsatisfactory. At least it would be lively and undemanding, though what she really needed was someone fully in the picture, someone she could unburden herself to without restraint. She was close to her sister in a way, but not really that way. In effect, the only possibilities were Den and Frances, and Marion felt paralysed with embarrassment at the idea of contacting them. For that matter, they had not been in touch with her either, since Nicol's departure. Rebecca had been chirpy and friendly, and Marion had to be happy about that. Otherwise she drifted in this limbo, empty, yet stressful, leading nowhere.

'That's what I like to hear. Keep busy, get out and about.' Jilly was taking her leave, waving her free hand. 'And don't forget, any time you feel lonely, you can always come and see us.'

'Thanks, Jill, I'll remember. I don't like to intrude, though.' *Not if I can help it, not on your tight little scene.*

'Don't be an idiot! We'd be glad to see you any

time. Must rush, love. Enjoy yourself—and don't brood. Nothing's worth it, whatever it is.'

'Goodbye, and give my best to . . .'

But Jilly was swinging away down the road, headed Brianwards and homewards, to the cosy privacy of real life. Marion strolled on, back straight, head high. She had full charge of her body, but her mind was a different proposition. The thoughts and feelings churned in an endless cycle, day and night.

Another weekend, then another week. Then another weekend. How many? For how long? Where were they pointing? Only to more and yet more of the same?

Oh, Nicol would reappear on the scene eventually, when it suited him, but then what? When he left, Marion had simply felt bleak, stunned, like a person who has been seduced and deceived. Twice bitten; a person who ought to have seen it coming, after the first time. Now she could see the whole escapade as a shared responsibility. Between them, they had successfully wedged themselves into a sharp corner. Whatever Nicol's complex motives, she had responded and acted, and she was a grown woman. She already regretted her upsurge of appalled anger, on making that shocking discovery—but she could not blame herself entirely. Wouldn't anyone have reacted that way? Wouldn't they have had every right to?

That night was marked by another ending, although of course it should have struck her as a relief, a new beginning. The end of one anxiety, but at the same time, the extinguishing of a tiny, foolish, irrational spark of hope. Ridiculous—preposterous—in her position, to actually welcome the very real possibility that she might be carrying Nicol's child within her! She was a sensible, busy schoolteacher, not some emotionally shallow schoolgirl. So, she had fallen heavily for Nicol: instantly been enmeshed in him. But the earthquake had not been destined to last, any more than that other affair had been. That time, she had taken such care; every precaution, reason before action. Somehow this time, no such level-headedness had interfered. Instinct had ruled the day; and ever since, instinct had built up its own illogical momentum of secret, guilty fantasy.

Now there was no easy way out. She wasn't pregnant, even if she might deserve to be. She was on her own—free, released—and firmly back in an impasse that needed adult measures, time, calm consideration, if it was to be resolved. When he finally bounced back, would Nicol have the sheer power to manoeuvre them out of this? Would he even try? Marion wasn't even sure whether she hoped so, or whether she dreaded the prospect of ever setting eyes on him again.

Marion never forgot the exact date when the letter arrived, because it was her birthday. November the nineteenth: a Tuesday. A morning like any other, when she grabbed her post as it came through the door and glanced at it over a quick breakfast before dashing to school.

Today there was a satisfying batch of cards, all shapes and sizes, small packages and loving messages, from friends, family . . . Marion smiled with pleasure. It was good to be remembered, even when one reached the sedate maturity of twenty-six. And for once there wasn't a single boring manilla envelope in amongst the greetings: no bills or tax forms to spoil the effect.

There was a strange one, though. Long, blue, lightweight. Festooned with bright alien stamps.

The date on the postmark claimed it had taken over a week to get here. From Mexico City.

Her name and address, in that same script she had seen on those postcards to Rebecca. Bold, black ink, thickly defined, rounded and upright. Cutting a dash, knowing what it wanted to say.

Marion stared at it. Time froze, and all the other envelopes slipped from her fingers, on to her lap. Her attention, her whole being, whittled itself down, crystallising on that one letter. In dreamy slow motion she carefully slit the top with a knife, automatically preserving the stamps for her nephew's collection; drew out the two thin, closely-covered white sheets.

She read it, then read it again. At first just words, lines, written to her by Nicol. Then gradually, meanings behind them, perhaps between them.

'Dear Marion,

This is not the time nor place for idle gossip—wish you were here, having a great trip, all that nonsense. I am either up to the eyes in archives, or up to the knees in muddy soil. Pursuing researches on an archaeological dig, where they kindly allow me access to their more significant Aztec finds. Wonderful!'

He presented such a vivid picture, Marion found herself smiling, trying at the same time to control a nervous tremor which had started up in her legs and hands.

'I have one—no, two, things to say to you. First, I appreciate your further help with Becky. I assume you to be wise. In view of recent events, you are also

generous. I know this because I've
managed a brief, crackly telephone call
to Frances, and she reports all exceedingly
well on that front.'

Rebecca had mentioned the excitement of a call
from her father: a rare occasion, when he was
tucked away in the more remote parts of an area. It
had been the highlight of the child's week, and
Marion had smilingly sympathised as the news had
poured out.

'R. has evidently recovered from her
self-imposed jolt, in fact according to
Fran, she is all the more relaxed since.
But what about you—the victim? I
perceive you to be tough outside and soft
inside. Please don't let the two polarise
each other so that you suffer. Let the
conflict out; let them merge. Believe me,
it hurts if you don't, and I know what
I'm talking about, otherwise I wouldn't
presume to offer you this advice. Why
should you, of all women, listen to me,
of all men?'

Marion was breathing heavily now, fingers clenched
round the edge of the letter. The words swam, yet
they were as clear as headlines in a newspaper.

'Second thing, and most important. I
have no time now for further reflections,
much as I regret that. But on Friday 22
November I shall arrive in England. I
will not be coming to London, nor even
telling F., D. and R. about my visit.
Please don't you mention it to them,

either. This is between you and me. I don't want Becky upset or disrupted when she's doing so well.'

No—well, he wouldn't. But in that case, why was he coming? Where? Whatdid it have to do with her? Marion closed her eyes, heaved a steadying sigh, and carried on.

'I shall go direct to the Swan Inn, near Banbridge, which is a tiny village not far from Henley-on-Thames. It's quiet, discreet, miles from anything except the river. And the food's excellent!'

Marion allowed herself a stiff grin, echoing the one which had surely accompanied this reference to their mutual interest in eating, as he wrote it, all of eight days earlier.

'Also, as you'll have worked out, it's a quick journey for me from Heathrow, and I don't intend to gad about once I get there. I intend to book us both in, you and I, under our own names, in separate rooms, for three nights. I must return to Mexico on the Monday.

'As you see, Marion, you are in no way compromised. You need not turn up, and if you do, nothing is taken for granted. But I'll be there. I have an urge to see you, touch you, talk to you. There are things I must tell you. I can't write them, and I can't wait till I'm officially back, amid Christmas cheer and general rejoicing.

'Look on this as a chance to make one

of your rare sorties from the city scrum.
An opportunity to test the public transport
system you're so keen on championing.
Or just as a weekend away from it all—
all except me, that is. I won't plead or
reason with you. But consider carefully,
my sweet, and come if you feel you can,
when you can. I won't phone—I'll simply
wait. If I don't see you, I'll just return. I
could do with a brief respite myself—a
spell of English peace, somewhere hassle-
free and conducive to quiet thought.'

His very description of the place, the calm
atmosphere—the notion of the two of them, alone
and anonymous, with time and space to sort
themselves out . . . Marion felt herself warming up
as she read it, but the tremor intensified in her
limbs all the same.

'Before I close, here's a nice little
quote to ponder on. Den once used it in
one of his sermons (you should go along
and hear one some time, if you haven't
already. I know you're not a devout
believer any more than I am, but I have
to say that my brother produces a fine
sermon). I forget where he said it came
from, though I did ask afterwards. One
of those eminent fellow-clergymen and
men of letters, about a hundred years
ago. He used it on purpose, for my sake,
because it seemed relevant to me at the
time. Now, for what it's worth, I pass it
on to you.
'*Every substantial grief has twenty*

*shadows, and most of them are shadows
of your own making.*

'Take care of yourself, Marion, as well
as of my wilful offspring. Remember that
Den and Frances are there, should
you need encouragement. Think of me,
looking behind and not ahead, in the
Mayan way. And hoping to see you, soon
if not sooner.

Yours, Nic.'

Marion read through the letter so many times,
she was late for school. She carried it about all day,
a pressing secret, drilling a burning hole in her
briefcase. In the evening, as soon as she gained the
privacy of her flat, she read it several times more.

Half the night, she tossed and muttered to herself.
In her head Nicol's voice, warm, persuasive, spoke
the words she now knew by heart. Words soothing
her, summoning her, with only two days' notice, to
a romantic tryst in a riverside hotel, west of London.

A mad suggestion, surely! But what lay behind
it? Did he really have these vital messages,
explanations perhaps, for her? Or was this just
another way of ensuring her continued devotion to
his daughter—so necessary, so desirable, for his
own peace of mind as well as Rebecca's? On the
face of it, that seemed more likely.

He was consolidating the work of those final few
minutes, nearly three weeks ago. Buttering her up.
He'd never really be there; he'd cancel it, any
moment now. How could it be worth it, flying back
from Central America just to spend two days—not
forgetting the three nights—with Marion, tucked
away in the depths of rural Oxfordshire?

And even if he had any intention of fulfilling this
dramatic promise, she'd be a fool to play along with

it. Crazy, even to consider meeting him there. Whatever he had to say to her, surely it could wait? He was bound to be home by Christmas, as he'd assured Rebecca. All this cloak and dagger stuff—whims and fancies, not Marion's world! For the second time in a fortnight, she reminded herself that she was a hard-headed professional woman, with two feet firmly on the ground, and better things to do than trek about the country in the middle of November, wasting precious weekend time on expeditions that would doubtless turn out to be fruitless. Fraught with risks, whether he actually materialised or not.

No, the proposition was outlandish. She'd better ignore it.

CHAPTER EIGHT

REACHING the Swan Inn, Banbridge, involved careful planning. A bus to Paddington; then two trains; finally the rare luxury of a taxi. It was early Friday evening by the time Marion stood on the gravelled drive, small holdall in one hand, staring up at the pretty stone building, subtly lit to show its coat of tangled ivy and wisteria. In the enveloping darkness it nestled among trees and fields, greens turned to mysterious greys; its gardens sloped down to where the Thames flowed—ancient, peaceful, purposeful.

Light poured from windows, and the heavy door stood welcomingly ajar. Marion drew in a long breath: no backing out now. She had not got up at seven this morning to pack, then rushed off as soon as afternoon school was over, only to suffer from cold feet at the last moment. Nicol had issued this challenge. She had risen to it, and for better or worse, here she was.

She walked through a warm lobby into a wide foyer, visibly leading to lounges and bars, thickly carpeted stairs, an atmosphere of cosy luxury; relaxed wellbeing. Much as she had envisaged from Nicol's description. He had such a way with words, whether speaking or writing, he brought everything to life with a new . . .

'Good evening. May I help you?'

The young blonde receptionist was ready with her bright smile and brighter voice.

'I believe you have a room booked in my name.'
Marion hesitated. 'A single room. Marion Thomas.'

The receptionist's practised eye scanned her list,
one manicured fingertip following its progress. It
stopped, and she looked up, her smile widening.
'We certainly have, Miss Thomas. Room 12. If
you'd just . . .'

Marion put her holdall down and advanced to
lean on the counter. So far, so good. Fantasy was
hardening to fact, and her confidence grew as she
began to trust it at last.

'I'm meeting a friend. He should have a room
booked as well.'

Her dark eyes were steady, but her own words
caused a flutter in her stomach. The receptionist
only went on smiling: well bred, well trained to give
nothing away. She was used to it all, that smile
implied: all sorts, all combinations, coming and
going past this highly polished wooden desk.

'That would be Mr Jarvis, the gentleman who
made the reservation by telephone from abroad.
Terrible line, I remember it was.' A delicate wrinkle
marred the smoothness of her brow. 'Where was he
calling from? I forget . . . somewhere exotic, I'm
sure it was . . .'

'Central America,' Marion informed her bluntly.

'That was it, Mexico City. How wonderful to visit
such exciting places!' The girl sighed dreamily. She
couldn't have been much over twenty. 'Have you
been there too, Miss Thomas?'

'I'm afraid not. I haven't travelled much.' *Even
coming here is an adventure for me, if you did but
know it . . .*

'You leave the globe-trotting to Mr Jarvis.' The
receptionist nodded understandingly. 'Well, your
friend is most efficient. We were all impressed. It
appears he stayed here some years ago, with . . .

before my time. Kind of him to remember us and make a point of returning.'

She covered her tiny slip so smoothly, Marion almost managed not to notice it. Unfortunately, she did notice it. Well, of course Nicol had been here before, otherwise how could he have recommended it with such deliberate confidence? But when—or with whom—Marion had never paused to consider. Now she was forced to, and the inner flutterings increased to anxious churnings. So, what if this was all part of a process of recapturing something he thought he'd lost . . . fitting her into a gap which had been cruelly torn in his life? He said he had to talk to her, put her straight about certain matters. Maybe this was the only place in the world he could do it. She must not jump to conclusions; she must school herself. Maybe . . .

'Miss Thomas?' The receptionist, a model of well-concealed impatience, leaned forward to arrest her wandering attention.

'I'm sorry.' Marion snapped back to the here and now.

'I was just saying, Mr Jarvis was very clever to remember us.'

'Mr Jarvis likes to get things right.' Marion's gaze was still direct, but her cheeks were flushed.

'I'm sure.' The receptionist was busy finding the right page in the register, then passing it to Marion over the counter. 'If you could just fill this in, Miss Thomas, please.'

'Oh . . . yes.' Marion fumbled in her handbag for a pen, but the girl was already pushing one across to her. 'Of course.'

The suspense was getting to her, but she couldn't bring herself to actually ask. Her eyes lifted, of their own accord, searching past the desk, through the foyer, towards the bustle of voices, movement—

the smells of food and drink—people enjoying a
sociable evening. Was he among them, waiting for
her?

Then her gaze fell, back to the register, the list of
names and addresses above hers. Was his there?
Had he already checked in?

'In case you were wondering, Mr Jarvis hasn't
arrived yet.'

For a brief moment, Marion's hand hovered over
the page. Then she went on writing her address.
When she had finished, she raised her head, put the
pen down and returned that level, slightly haughty
stare. 'No, well, he wouldn't have; he's got a lot
further to come than me.'

'That's true. Plenty of time yet.'

Marion picked up her case. 'So I'll go on up to
my room, if that's okay with you.' It was really
quite a relief. Now she'd have a chance to shower
and change so that she'd be prepared to greet him,
refreshed and poised, when he did appear.

'Right.' Reaching behind her, the receptionist
unhooked a key from its panel and handed it to
her. 'It's on the first floor. If you'll just wait a
second, Mr Deacon will show you up there and
carry your bag.' The groomed hand was on the
point of ringing a bell which stood at one end of
the counter.

'Good heavens, there's no need for that! I've
carried it all the way from London and it hardly
weighs a thing. Surely I can lug it up a few stairs!'

'Just as you like, Miss Thomas.' The girl was
imperturbable. 'You should find everything you
need. Any problems or queries, just lift the
telephone. Dinner's being served now, up to
midnight. Would you like me to call up to you
when Mr Jarvis arrives?' she added sweetly, as

Marion turned to go. 'He'll be in Room 10, next door.'

Marion swung back, arrested by a softening of tone, and perhaps a gleam of humour, even sympathy. For the first time she allowed herself a cautious but genuine grin. 'Not a bad idea. Would you?'

'I certainly would. You settle in, Miss Thomas. Plenty of hot water. No one will disturb you without warning.'

'Thanks.' Marion nodded briskly, then marched up the plush staircase, easily found the door marked 12 (and the one marked 10 beside it), let herself into the pleasant, well-appointed room, and set about the job of becoming comfortable and presentable. Plenty of hot water . . . plenty of time. Yes, that receptionist was more than just an ornament. Those were the best ingredients for inducing a state of dignified calm, in order to confront whatever lay ahead.

By nine forty-five, she had been ready for half an hour. She sat in the one small armchair, making a pretence at reading her newspaper, but every sense was alert for the sound of the room telephone. Her window gave on to the back of the hotel, so there was no advance notice of cars arriving at the front.

Suspense swelled in her, but no real concern. Nicol had to make a flight half-way around the world. He could hardly be expected to get here on the dot.

By ten-thirty she was clenching up, and the telephone remained obdurately mute. Marion's insides, on the other hand, were rumbling irritably. She'd eaten very little all day. There was no point in sliding into a state of depletion while she waited for Nicol. But should she summon room service and demand a sandwich, or brave the restaurant on her

own? She was not used to such decisions: she'd had
virtually no experience of doing either. Hands
clasped in her lap, fingers twisted together, she
perched on the edge of the chair.

In her head, she had lectured herself—all the last
two days, all the way here—that he might let her
down . . . be late . . . not turn up. In her heart, she
knew better. He would be here, as he had promised.

By ten forty-five, she was pacing the room, all
semblance of philosophical patience abandoned. She
palpitated and sweated; her temples were beginning
to tighten and throb. Damn! Just as she had got
herself all balanced and sorted out, this had to
happen! Jerkily she grabbed the receiver by the
bed.

'This is Room 12. I wondered . . .' She adjusted
her voice, which sounded strangely squeaky. 'I
wondered if . . .'

'Hallo, Miss Thomas. No sign of Mr Jarvis yet,
I'm afraid.'

'It wasn't that. I...'

'I'd convey any message to you directly I received
it.'

'I know you would. Thanks.' With an effort,
Marion contrived a note of nonchalance. 'I wanted
to ask about something to eat.'

'You must be starving!' The receptionist was
positively friendly now. 'Why don't you come down
and have a bite, to tide you over? You don't have
to have the full meal, you know. We do bar snacks
too. Very good ones.'

'Would you send something up here?'

'Of course. But . . .' she seemed to hesitate, then
reach a decision. 'You don't really want to stay in
your room by yourself, do you? I'm due to go off
duty very soon. Why don't you join me for a snack,
and maybe a glass of wine, on the house? While

you wait for Mr Jarvis to arrive? I expect his plane's been delayed, don't you? He wouldn't want you to fade away with hunger just because he was late,' she pointed out practically.

'No. Well . . .' It was a generous suggestion, kindly meant. A very human face lurked behind that bland, sophisticated front. Marion quickly made up her mind. 'Yes, I'll do that, thanks. I must say, I'm ravenous. And I could do with a drink,' she admitted, throwing the last shred of spurious reserve to the winds. This was a fellow-female, surely an ally, even if she had no clue what was really at stake. Who was Marion to refuse any offer of support in a tense situation?

'I'll see you down here in five minutes, then, shall I?'

'Yes. Thank you.'

'Not at all. I often have a nightcap before I turn in. Mr Deacon takes over at eleven. It'll be nice to have a bit of company. I'm not really supposed to fraternise with the guests too much, but once in a while I make an exception.' She chuckled. 'And if anything's calculated to bring your friend, ordering some supper without him will do it! Isn't it always the way?'

Marion was so grateful, she even laughed. 'I suppose so.'

She bathed her burning face and hands in cool water, combed out her hair all over again, stepped into her best shoes, locked her door and made her way downstairs. This girl was right again. She was like an internal commentator—the conscious voice of Marion's own submerged thoughts. You had to get on with life from stage to stage, take care of the minutes and the hours would look after themselves. Stupid not to provide for her body's basic needs, even if the rest of her cried for a deeper fulfilment.

She needed to be at top strength when Nicol did finally join her.

It was well past midnight when she struggled down from her high stool, caught at the edge of the bar for support, swayed slightly and blinked. That fourth glass of hock might perhaps have been one glass too many, with only the chicken sandwich to absorb it. A very acceptable chicken sandwich, in fresh granary bread, with home-made mayonnaise and crisp lettuce, followed by a cup of good coffee and two thin chocolate mints—but still, apparently, not enough to prevent a certain—how could she put it . . . wooziness creeping over her.

'Better get some rest,' she confided to her companion. The words were mildly slurred, but at least she felt reasonably relaxed. Or dulled—protected from reality—that might express it better. 'Had a long day,' she explained. 'Teaching the brats, then travelling, then . . .'

'Then the waiting. I know. You go to bed, Miss Thomas. He'll probably get here in the middle of the night and you'll see him in the morning.'

'Marion. I'm Marion.' It seemed ridiculous: she knew all about this person's family in Epsom, her handsome boy-friend, away at college learning to be an expert on computers, her sojourn at one of the most expensive girls' schools in England (a riot, if her accounts were to be credited)—and she didn't know her name.

'And I'm Henry.'

'Did you say Henry?' Marion blinked again.

'That's what I said. Awful, isn't it? But my real name's even worse: Henrietta.' She grimaced. 'So on the whole, I prefer Henry. Believe it or not, I used to be quite a tomboy when I was a kid. Climbing trees, riding horses and all that.'

'I like it. Hen . . . Henri . . . Henrietta.' For

some reason it took a bit of saying. 'Well, thanks, Henry. For the drink and—and . . .'

'It's a pleasure, Marion. I told you, I often unwind here before I go to bed. It seemed silly, you being hungry all alone, and me snacking in solitary splendour. Especially after most of the other customers have gone home, or up to their rooms.'

'Mmm.' Marion's head reeled. She really was exhausted.

Henry reached out to take her arm. 'Come on, I'll make sure you don't land up in the wrong room. Might give some bloke a pleasant shock, but this hotel's keen on preserving its good name.'

Marion giggled as they set off, padding together across soft carpets through discreetly lit corridors. 'Where do you sleep, Henry?' She enunciated extra clearly in case tiredness was causing her to mumble.

'I've got a cell in the west wing. Servants' quarters.'

Outside her door, Marion scrabbled for her key. 'Will you be around in the morning?'

'I don't go on duty till after lunch, so I might get up late, but I'll be around.' She patted Marion's hand. A few hours ago, the gesture would have seemed insulting, but now it was reassuring. Amazing what a lot could happen (and not happen) in a few hours. 'You get some sleep. If he turns up in the small hours, Mr Deacon will show him straight to his room. More likely, he'll have been so delayed, he's spending the night at the airport or something.'

'Yes. Well then, I'll catch up on some rest.'

'That's the way. He's bound to arrive at some unearthly hour.'

Even in her fuddled state, Marion recognised when someone was going all out to encourage her.

She wished she could be so sure. 'Goodnight, then. Thanks again, Henry.'

Henry waved a dismissive hand, tossed back her long fair hair, and was gone. Marion brushed her teeth, changed into her new nightdress—pale yellow, in softest filmy cotton lawn, flowing and lacy—and climbed between pristine sheets.

Worn out, she drifted for a while, just above sleep, just below full awareness. Of course Henrietta was right. Even now, Nicol was winging his way in her direction. Eastwards through the high thin dark air, following the sunrise. He was bound to arrive, at some unearthly hour. Bound to.

Seven hours later she awoke suddenly, and lay marshalling the flood of feelings which immediately swamped her. The slight headache, the twinge of nausea, deserved effects of last night's indulgence. Then the bewilderment; realisation; hope; fear. They shifted and merged in a mind still drugged from sleep.

She could tell by the sharp light edging round the curtains that it was a fine morning. But could she sense, by the vibrations coming through the interconnecting wall, whether Nicol had arrived in the night and was asleep in that next room? Or was it as empty, as optimistically waiting, as she was herself?

She closed her eyes again, bracing herself, either way. No mystic message reached her across the airwaves. She'd have to get up, go downstairs and find out.

This time it was a man behind the desk: middle-aged, spruce. Doubtless the legendary Mr Deacon, proprietor of this establishment. He greeted her with a courteous smile.

'Good morning. I hope you slept well, Miss—er—Mrs . . .?'

'Thomas. Room 12. Yes, thank you. Any sign of my friend, Mr Jarvis?' There was no point in prevaricating: she had to know.

'Ah yes, Mr Jarvis. Made the booking all the way from Mexico.' This had obviously gone down in the annals of the hotel as a major event. Marion fought back her suspense, as he glanced down Henry's list, then at the panel of keys. 'No sign at all, I'm afraid, No message either.' He frowned. 'Strange—we'd have heard by now if there was a serious hitch at that end—weather or something. Shall I telephone the airport and check, Miss Thomas?'

'If you would.' A tough strand of resignation tempered her bitter disappointment; the beginnings of disillusion. 'I'm going to have some breakfast. Please let me know what they say.'

At a small table, in single state among a few other hushed morning diners, she ate her way through fresh grapefruit, scrambled eggs, toast and marmalade, and drank tea. Then she went back to the foyer. Mr Deacon looked up and shook his head.

'Both flights from Mexico City were on time yesterday. No problems with conditions. Mr Jarvis was on the passenger list of the morning flight, but evidently was not on the plane. That's all they can say.'

Marion swallowed hard, as a solid lump formed in her throat. 'Well, thank you for your trouble. Please let me know if you hear anything.'

'He knows you're here, doesn't he?' Mr Deacon was solicitous. 'He'll get in touch, I'm sure, and explain why he's been held up.'

'I expect so.' She plodded back to her room, slowly, stair by stair. How to fend off this mounting

sense of bitterness? A skim of self-protective
cynicism was already setting, like a mix of plaster,
on her soul. Hours stretched ahead, and they
weren't just lonely; they were strung out with a
tension that rocked back and forth, back and forth.
Praying he would come; hoping he wouldn't after
all. As time passed, Marion was becoming more
confused about which she really wanted.

Later, she forced herself into action—no use
sitting stupidly in this impersonal room, better to
keep on the move—and took herself out for a walk.
There was still no Henry in the offing, so she
handed her key to Mr Deacon and set off through
the lush grounds; lawns, then copses and woods,
down to the river bank.

It was all so tranquil on this translucent late
autumn day. The perfect setting, just as Nicol had
prescribed. *English peace . . . quiet, discreet, miles
from anything except the river*. Oh yes, it would
have been wonderful to share this place, this day
with Nicol. He could have said anything here, done
anything. *I have this urge to see you, touch you . . .*

Marion stopped to stare at the sluggish flow of
the Thames: soothing and hypnotic. She had
believed he meant it; she must go on believing. She
must have faith; there was still time. The rest of
today . . . tomorrow . . . he had been unavoidably
delayed, that was all.

She returned quickly to the hotel. It was chilly,
despite the clear air, and Henry would soon be on
duty. It was time for a cup of coffee and a snack . . .
perhaps there would be news, in her absence . . .

There was no news, but Henry was ensconced
behind the desk, back to her glamorously efficient
self.

'Don't worry.' She handed Marion her key, with
a smile, still amiable and supportive. 'Give it time.'

'I've got no choice, really, have I?' Marion stayed to chat for a while, but Henry was very busy today, so she spent the afternoon browsing through glossy magazines by an open fire in one of the lounges. Her ear was permanently cocked for a familiar voice or a call; her whole body stiffened each time she heard a telephone. Nothing happened. No one called her, no one came looking for her.

She began to feel stirrings of panic. She was in such a strange kind of isolation here: no one knew where she was—except Nicol. These people were kind enough, and Henry was really sweet, but they neither knew nor cared about her real self. To them, she was just another guest, with a more-than-usually unenviable problem, but not one they could do anything about. To them, it must look like a classic plot: a romantic tryst between two friends in a country hotel. A *broken* romantic tryst.

She winced, and viciously turned over several pages of impossibly glitzy advertisements. She wasn't bothering them, not even Henry, with details. She had got here on her own, and she would cope on her own, whether Nicol deigned to show up or not.

By early evening the place was livening up. Saturday night, of course, bound to be one of their busiest. Dinner guests arrived, smart loving couples sitting at intimate candleglowing tables, just to add to Marion's chagrin. There was live music—a piano trio in one restaurant—and revellers jostling in both bars.

Refusing to skulk in her room, Marion watched it all from a corner of the lounge, evading eye contact with anyone as she munched another solitary sandwich. It was an object lesson in just how alone one can feel among a happy crowd. In fact, the happier and more crowded, the lonelier one felt.

Especially when one hadn't expected, or chosen, to be there alone.

Tonight she kept off the wine, determined to maintain a clear head—to conquer this rising stress without resorting to the dulling action of alcohol, tempting as it was.

She crept up to her room early, without speaking to Henry, who was fully occupied supervising arrivals and departures. Might as well get some rest. Waiting in suspense was the most tiring process in the world. There was still every chance he might arrive, even now.

On Sunday everything started later and went on at a lower key, as if the whole place needed to recuperate from Saturday's exertions. There was nothing from Nicol. Not a whisper.

Marion went for another walk. It was colder today, windy, with billowing rain-filled clouds. But still bracingly beautiful, here in rural England. Exactly what Nicol had said he needed. The ideal setting for a meeting, a coming together . . .

As she marched back across the grounds, hands in coat pockets, skin pink from air and exercise, Marion at last gave way to the turmoil at the heart of her control. An underlying emotion had seethed, just below the surface, all this time, only waiting to erupt as anticipation had turned to apprehension, then disappointment, finally resentment.

Anger. A rekindling of that earlier fury, a part of her nature since infancy; her surest defence in times of desertion and pain. Sheer blind rage brought her storming back now into the warm confines of the building; sent her stamping upstairs to her room; guided her shaking hands as they automatically threw things into her holdall. Cold fury carried her down to the foyer again, even permitted her a frozen apology for a smile at Henry as she requested her bill, wrote out a cheque and slid it across the desk without another word.

'Not even staying for something to eat?' On duty, Henry was far too tactful to probe, but her expression spoke volumes. *The bastard! How dare he stand you up! Men—who needs 'em!*

Marion was too far gone to be mollified. Stiffly she picked up her bag; her cheeks burned but her chin was held high. 'No, I'll get off now. I'll have something on the train. I can't hang about here all day—I have to be at work in the morning. I might have stayed tonight,' she added, perhaps to herself, her tone dropping, 'if . . . but . . .'

'He might still make it.' Suddenly conspiratorial, since no one else was looking, Henry leaned across the counter. 'What shall I say if he does, or if he calls?'

'Tell him I came, that's all. He knows where to find me.'

'No other message?' Henry was more intrigued than she had been letting on. She was quite a connoisseur of other people's clandestine affairs, discreet two-night stands, by now, and in her opinion there was nothing sordid, or even temporary, about how this Thomas woman felt.

'No. No other message.' Marion turned to go. Then, remembering something, she turned back. 'Thanks for helping me through that first evening, Henry. It was good to know someone was there . . . you know . . .'

'I enjoyed your company. I'm sorry it didn't work out, Marion.'

Marion stared at her a moment, then shrugged. 'Better go, I suppose. I'm walking into Banbridge—it'll do me good. The bus leaves for Twyford in half an hour, according to that timetable you've got on

the wall. I should be in time for the London
connection from there.'

'Take care, then.' Henry was holding Marion's
cheque between both hands, surveying her over the
top of it as if she might decipher some truth behind
this sad story unfolding for her benefit, like a soap
opera on television. At the same time, only too
ordinary: real life.

'You too.' Marion waved as she made for the
door.

'I'm sorry, Marion.' There was a note of urgency
in Henry's final words, echoing after her as she
walked down the drive. Almost as if it had been
Henry's fault! Marion smiled grimly.

Sorry! Not half as sorry as Marion was! She'd
been a sucker to get herself into this mess. It had
promised to be one of the most rewarding weekends
of her life—positive and exciting, at the very least—
and it had turned out to be the worst.

Perhaps Nic had meant to come. Perhaps not.
Even if he had—even if some inescapable hurdle
had detained him—he might have had the common
decency to let her know. Taking all that trouble,
writing to her, making the booking from so far
away—then nothing. Not even the simple courtesy,
the favour of a second-hand message.

Marion narrowed her eyes on to the road. Tears
threatened, somewhere in the depths of them, and
she needed her wits about her now, with a journey
ahead. Doubtless she'd come to see it as a blessing
in disguise, his failure to keep the appointment. A
signal to his true character: unreliable, volatile,
behind all that winning self-expression. A nailing of
colours to the mast.

And in the nick of time too, before she fell so far
in there was no hauling her out. Before she
committed herself and her unstable emotions to . . .

God knew what . . . some irrevocable action, or decision . . .

Shuddering, she quickened her pace along the quiet road. Yes, she had probably been let off lightly. He had thought better of the whole thing—and so should she have done, if she'd had any sense.

The anger writhed and twisted away inwards, aiming away from Nicol and into herself, darkening to a deep private shame. The most anguishing rage of all: self-recrimination. During the slow trip home, it solidified like concrete. She arrived weary, bleak, wiped out. The empty flat was soundless. The telephone sat in the hall, bellowing its silence.

No letter or telegram or note on the mat, either. So it was over. The episode that never was.

CHAPTER NINE

As FAR as the children were concerned, December
meant only one thing: Christmas. By the time the
month was a few days old, every classroom was
festooned and glittering. Trees, stars, paper chains,
tinsel—the whole school was in bright seasonal mood,
from headmaster down to tiniest nursery fledgling.

The effect of all this on Marion was enervating. A
mockery of her own, persistent sense of flat anticlimax.
At least this year her class was not participating in
the Nativity play, but some of them were playing and
singing in a carol concert, and there was no evading
her share in that. Knowing just how exciting it was
for them, she did her level best to enter superficially
into the spirit of the occasion. If she often felt
sombre, and sometimes downright churlish, she was
too controlled—and too sincerely attached to her
charges—to let them see it.

It was a Wednesday lunchtime when she was called
to the Secretary's Office. An urgent message arrived
at the staff room door, delivered by a self-important
fourth-year prefect. Marion made her way quickly
along the corridor and up the stairs, not wanting to
be late for the start of afternoon lessons.

'Joan?' She pushed the office door open. 'You sent
for me?'

'Oh yes, Marion, come on in.' The school secretary
made a point of appearing harassed but actually being
highly organised. 'Telephone call for you—important.
Promised I'd convey the gist to you straight away.'

150

She rummaged among the heaps of paper around her typewriter.

'Call, for me?' Marion's heartrate quickened. Who could be contacting her here? And why? She took two steps towards the desk.

'Yes.' Glancing up, Joan noticed the tension in her face. 'It's all right; nothing dire. Not even personal. It's about one of your little angels . . . now let me see . . . where the hell did I put that note . . .'

'Ah!' One of her pupils—that was nothing to worry about. It did happen, though rarely: a concerned parent with some crucial information to impart, unwilling to write or come in person. 'Which of my . . .?'

'Here we are!' Triumphantly, Joan waved a scrap of paper adorned with a few squiggles. 'Rebecca Jarvis, that's the child.'

'Rebecca?' Marion winced as if she had been flicked by a stinging fingertip.

'Don't look so worried!' Joan peered at her over half-moon spectacles. 'Take it easy, Marion! Have you been overworking? Must be the time of year. Cool it, as my sons would say. Hang loose.'

'Sorry.' Sinking into the chair opposite Joan, Marion even plucked a smile from some inner reserve. 'Just that Rebecca's been a lot better lately, and today she's particularly happy—getting nicely steamed up about playing her recorder in *We Three Kings*, but otherwise really quite . . .'

'Well, I hope she'll stay that way. But I gather there's some minor family crisis, and this uncle—the clergyman, what's his name, the Reverend Mr Jarvis, I suppose . . .' She tried to decipher her own scrawl.

'Denham Jarvis. Yes.' It took all Marion's willpower to conceal this mounting sick anxiety; worse, because she barely understood it.

'That's him. Vicar of St Peter's, I believe? Anyway,

he wants to see you, that's the point. As soon as possible, to talk about this . . . whatever it is, before they tell the girl. Keeping you in the picture, I'd guess, after the trouble you've taken.' Joan sighed. 'I hope it's not gloomy tidings. Hasn't she got an adventurous father, away in foreign parts?'

'She has.' *Nothing dire*, Joan had chanted cheerfully; *nothing personal*. What did *she* know? 'So when does he want to see me?'

'He's looking in at the end of school today. I said I'd be gone by four, and you can use this office. No one will disturb you. Can you spare him a few minutes? I'm sure it won't take long.'

'Certainly.' Marion stood up. The sooner she got this afternoon's show on the road, the sooner it would be over. 'I'll be here. If he arrives first, Joan, please ask him to wait.'

'Of course. And I'll leave that file on the desk in case you need to refer to it. When you leave, please put it in this drawer, okay? Then lock the door and hand the key in to Mr Russell, on your way past his den, if you don't mind.'

'Will do. Thanks for the message. That was the bell, wasn't it? Better get along there now, or bedlam will break out.'

'Bedlam? In Miss Thomas's classroom? Never!'

But Marion was already through the door and walking away—fast, every muscle stretched taut, face clamped into position for the next two hours.

Den was waiting when she arrived back in the office just after four. His comfortable form, unfolding itself from Joan's swivel chair, should have been comforting, but it was not. That ambience—those features—were too familiar. Too reminiscent of recent discoveries and disappointments. She knew now why she had gone out of her way to avoid confronting it, this past fortnight.

He extended his hand and half-rose as she approached the desk.

'Marion, good to see you again. How've you been?'

'Not so bad, thanks, Den. And you, and the family?'

'We're all fine. Fine.' He hesitated before sitting down again. 'You must know how grateful Fran and I are for your miracles with Becky.'

'Mine?' Marion's smile was wry. 'I think you had rather more to do with that. You and Fran, and . . .'

'And Nicol. Yes, indeed. After he'd been home, she did seem to turn a corner and she's been making strides ever since. It's really because of that I'm here now.' His tone sharpened.

Up to now, she had evaded his eye—through embarrassment, or inhibition, or perhaps fear of what she might see in it. Now she glanced into his face, and saw a clear strain there. 'How do you mean?'

'We've had some news.'

'To do with—her father?'

'With Nic, yes.' If Marion had difficulty voicing his name, his brother did not.

She had no way of guessing how much Den knew of her involvement with Nicol. She clasped her hands, moist palms together. 'You've heard from him, then?'

'In a manner of speaking.' Suddenly Den was leaning towards her. 'Have you heard at all, Marion?'

'I've had one letter.'

'May I ask when?' His tone tightened again, pressing.

'I can't remember the date it was written, but I received it on my birthday. November the nineteenth.'

'Nothing since?' Den's face grew even more troubled, and Marion's insides clenched up in direct proportion.

'No, not a word.' There was a grimness in the acknowledgement: not a glimpse, not a squeak.

'So. Well.' Breathing deeply, he folded his arms across his chest. As a priest he was used to most kinds of demanding situations, but this one affected him deeply. Some remote corner of Marion's mind, aloof from the whirlpool of emotion filling the rest of it, told her he wasn't finding this any easier than she was. 'We had a telephone call, yesterday,' he said at last.

'Oh really?' Her response was studiously polite. *That's more than I did.* 'From Mexico?'

'Not directly. Not from him. About him. He's in hospital.' Coming to the point at last, Den blurted it out, moving abruptly forward in his chair, voice rising.

'Hospital?' Marion half-stood, then slumped down again. Redness, then blackness, invaded her eyes. Steadying herself, she closed them. 'What . . . why?' she whispered, her hands unconsciously groping towards Den: towards anyone, anything firm to hold on to.

He seemed unsurprised by the violence of her reaction. In fact, it seemed to harden his own resolve, and he became sympathetic yet blunt as he gave her the details. 'There was a serious accident, Marion. We only heard through his publishers in London, who heard it from their New York office, who heard it from their affiliated company in Mexico City. By the time it reached us, it was almost two weeks out of date. God only knows what might be happening now, but then . . .'

'What kind of accident?' Marion was muttering, terrified to know, but yearning to hear. Suddenly, knowing this was far more important than preserving her dignity, or her privacy, or any other part of her insignificant self. 'Tell me . . . please!'

Den studied her briefly, nodded and seemed almost to relax. 'He was driving a jeep . . . I don't know . . . some kind of Land Rover, or one of those hairy jobs they use, out in the desert or whatever rugged terrain he was trekking over at the time.'

'The dig? The project he was visiting?' Marion prompted him, breathlessly—avid, as if by knowing the full story she could magically influence its outcome.

'Right. As far as we can gather, somewhere out near Lake Chapala. Anyway, he was alone in this vehicle and it hit a massive bump or dip, and—over it went. Right over. Nic was thrown against the windscreen and . . .' Den was watching her carefully now, to see how she was taking it. 'And knocked out. Badly cut about the face. Fractured skull, they said. Concussed.'

'Oh no!' It was all so matter-of-fact, yet the image printing itself on her mind was so appalling: Nic with his head split open, blood, glass splinters . . . pale as death, eyes closed . . .

Marion leaned back in her chair. Her own eyelids drooped; her skin was as pallid, as clammy, as her vision of his.

Den was a sensitive man, and he had got the worst over. He became more gentle, but there was more to be said. 'He's been in a coma. He hadn't come round yet when they called us. They didn't even know where the hospital was, exactly—somewhere out in the sticks, but I'm sure he's being taken care of . . . we're doing all we can to find out . . .'

'But—but he will come round? He'll be all right?' she pleaded, as if Den could make it all right just by saying yes.

'I wish I knew. Might be brain damage, from a percussive blow like that; might not. If it's really a

fracture, things won't look too good. Evidently
there's always a chance, but . . .'

'How much of a chance, Den?' Astonishingly, she
was alert. Sheer shock held her together, and she
fired the questions like a round of bullets at the
poor man: Nic's brother, surely no less anguished
than she was herself.

He shrugged. 'Fifty/fifty. Depends how long
before he regains consciousness. If he does. We've
pestered all the doctors we know, and they say the
same. It's in . . .' he paused, spreading his hands,
'the hands of God,' he concluded, with no trace of
satire or cynicism.

'I see.' It was beginning to sink in, and with it,
some other home truths started filtering through as
well. 'When did it happen?'

'About November twentieth, I think. It took over
a week for the report to percolate to Mexico City.
It's pretty remote where he was, and communications
are lousy there at the best of times, what with
earthquakes and things. Then it took another few
days to relay it to New York, then on here. That's
why we only heard yesterday.'

Marion had buried her face in trembling hands.
Den would expect her to be stunned, but he couldn't
know the half of it. It had happened the day after
she'd received Nic's letter; two days before he was
due to fly out and join her. When he had failed to
materialise, Marion had gone through all the
possibilities, tortured herself with all the
conclusions—except the right one. She'd been so
paranoid, so stubbornly determined to feel victim-
ised, deceived, abandoned, that the most obvious
and most tragic explanation had totally eluded her.

It wasn't that he had thought better of it. Nor
that he was dropping her like the proverbial hot
brick. He wasn't letting her down, or playing games

with her. Just because some men did that, it didn't mean they all did.

No, he would have been there—but he was lying unconscious in a hospital bed in the wilds of Central America, with a cracked head, and who knew what other ghastly injuries. All that life and liveliness, that vigour and vitality . . . the warmth of words, gestures, experiences that were uniquely him . . . ebbing from him, perhaps leaving him empty, nothing but a dried-out husk of the man . . .

Marion could not bear it. And yet she had to. She had to raise her eyes to meet Den's, without flinching, and make herself say, 'I'm so very sorry, Den. It's terrible. And of course, you'll want my support, if and when you tell Rebecca?'

He nodded gratefully. 'We knew you'd understand. Fran was afraid you'd be too hurt, but I said . . .'

'You must think of Becky, put her first. And you were right.'

'You're a credit to your trade, Marion.' His appreciation widened to admiration. 'If we don't get positive news, one way or the other, we really don't know what to tell Becky. How long should we leave it?'

Now he was consulting her, not just as an interested party but as a mature professional, with valuable advice to offer. Responding, Marion found herself able to consider calmly, from all angles, and then reply. 'She's expecting him back for Christmas, right?'

'Right.'

'And not expecting to hear from him much before that?'

'He sends the odd card, occasionally phones, but not often. She wouldn't worry if she didn't hear. As long as we—you know—keep smiling, don't let on there's anything wrong.'

'Yes.' That would be the hardest and greatest responsibility, for all of them. Keeping a surface free of fear and fret, however much the anxiety seethed beneath. 'I don't think we should say anything at all,' Marion stated decisively. 'We should carry on as normally as we can . . . find out whatever we can . . . until it becomes inevitable to tell her. If nothing happens by Christmas, then— well then . . .'

She was strong; stronger than she'd ever dreamed she could be—for Nicol's sake, and Becky's, and for the sake of her own peace of mind—to make up for all that futile, self-gratifying fuming. Here was a grief that was real, elemental, and Marion was going to show what she was really made of.

But even this new-found strength had its limits, and now she ducked her head, and held her two fists against her hot cheeks, helpless as the tears finally rolled down—even welcoming the cleansing release of them. Den was on his feet at once, round the desk beside her. One hand rested on her shoulder; his concerned face close to hers. Marion's display of inner spirit had, in its turn, restored his own.

'You're absolutely right! We'll do that. We'll take it from day to day. You're wise, Marion; we thought so, and Nicol said . . .'

She lifted a tearstained face and stared into eyes that were a heartrending echo of Nic's. 'What? What did he say?'

Den stepped back, leaning on the wall. Again he seemed to reflect before reaching a decision. 'You know, don't you, that you bear an extraordinary likeness to his late wife? The one who . . .'

'Andrea, who drowned. Oh yes, I know.' But she gazed at him, eager to hear what he had to say.

'Thanks to Becky. Poor kid, not her finest hour,' Den observed drily. 'Anyway, I wasn't intending to mention it today, but in view of . . . all this . . . you might like to know what Nic said to us about that . . .'

'I would,' Marion assured him.

'It may be there, this resemblance. It *is* there, we all noticed it straight away. We were fascinated. But, Marion, it's only skin deep. A shadow, nothing more. A trick of the light.' Den chose his words with great care. 'If Nic was intrigued by you as a result of it, initially, any subsequent attraction was . . .' He was becoming stilted, in the effort to get it right. 'Was in spite of it rather than because of it. If he liked you, it wasn't for that reason. I can't explain properly now, Marion, and it's not really my place to, but perhaps one day Nic will tell you more himself.'

And perhaps not. 'I'm glad to know that much. Thank you for being so honest about it. I must admit, I was upset, when I found out.'

'The child meant it for the best. Nicol should have—would have told you, in his own good time . . .' Den was wiping his brow, then blowing his nose, with a voluminous handkerchief. 'I wasn't looking forward to this, but I must say, you've amazed me. We owe you a lot already, but after this, Marion . . .'

'Nonsense!' But this time, she had learned better than to claim she was only doing her job. She had learned a great deal more than that. 'You know I'm deeply involved with them both—Nicol, and Becky.' She gazed at him gravely before continuing. 'There's no point in pretending I don't care what happens to them, is there? I fell in love with your brother, almost as soon as I met him. I'll never be the same, now I've known him, whatever . . . whatever . . .' her voice cracked.

Den's hand was on her arm again. 'None of us will, Marion,' he interrupted softly. 'He has that effect. But we won't give up hope yet, eh? Tomorrow might bring better news—who knows?'

He squeezed her arm, and she recovered sufficiently to smile weakly and struggle to her feet. 'Who knows? Keep me in touch, won't you? Anything you hear, you'll let me know? I won't say a word to Becky—it'll be difficult, but I'll behave as normally as I can. Only please . . .'

'The moment we hear anything, we'll tell you, and that's a promise.'

They surveyed one another, and there was a very real bond between them, with Nicol's shape at the heart of it. Then Den was grinning valiantly, slightly maniacally, in a deliberate attempt to defuse the trauma.

'Shall I tell you something that might amuse you, before we go?'

She recognised his bid to prepare them both for the outside world, and she was grateful. 'About Nic?'

'Yes. I bet he hasn't told you this. Did you know that when he was a small boy, he had the most awful stammer?'

'*Nicol* did?'

'That's right. Up to—oh, I don't know, his early teens at least. It was all he could do to spit out two words at a time.'

'Good lord!' That most fluent, potent speaker . . . teller of tales, weaver of verbal spells?

'I know.' Even at such a moment, Den was relishing her incredulity. 'You see, he's left-handed.'

Marion did a double-take. 'I knew that. Like Rebecca. But why . . .?'

'If you make a naturally left-handed person use their right hand, as they sometimes insisted in our generation, it can lead to speech impediments and all sorts of other imbalances. Where we were brought up, in the Scottish backwoods, they didn't know any better, and they forced Nic to do everything with his right hand. When we moved to London, the new school suggested letting him do his own thing, the way he instinctively wanted—and lo!' He waved a majestic arm.

Marion had to smile through her pain, at this glimpse of the vicar in his pulpit. 'Lo?'

'Lo and behold, the stammer gradually disappeared. The more he was allowed to use his left hand, the less difficulty he had making himself understood. Fortunately, it wasn't too late.'

Marion was riveted. 'That could explain a lot about him.'

'It does. He's been a born communicator ever since. It was like releasing an avalanche of word-power which had been stored up for years, and it's never stopped flowing. As if he constantly has to prove his articulacy—never been absolutely certain of it—always drawing you in, with language and ideas.'

'Drawing you in.' Marion sighed and nodded. Yes, she had been drawn in, willingly captivated. Words and ideas were the ropes which had drawn her; physical and emotional warmth were the meshes which had ensnared her. Now he was missing, but the ropes went on tugging and the net ensnaring, and doubtless they always would, even if she never saw or heard him again.

She pushed her untidy hair back from her flushed face, in an effort to get herself together. 'I certainly didn't know that, but then I didn't know much about him, really.' *Nothing; everything.*

'Thought you might be interested.' Den picked up his coat. 'Well, we'd best be off. Walking down the road with me?'

'Please. I've just got to lock this folder away . . .' That Jarvis file: she'd written nothing in it. At this moment she'd be hard put to lift a pen, let alone write a sensible word; but given time she'd scribble some sketchy note to show that her professional self had attended this interview, not just her real one.

They parted on the street corner. 'Give my love to Fran and the little ones. And don't forget to keep in touch, Den.'

'We will, don't worry. We need you, to keep a watchful eye on Becky.'

'You can trust me, I won't let her down.'

'No. We appreciate that, and so would—will Nicol,' he corrected himself emphatically. 'I'll make some enquiries tomorrow, see if I can't track him down more satisfactorily, but it does seem to be a horrendous place to try and contact anyone.'

'We'll all do what we can.' Marion shifted from one foot to the other. 'Coming to hear Becky sing and play at the concert?'

'You bet! Top priority. Last day of term, isn't it?'

'Friday the twentieth, that's right.'

'We'll see you before that, I hope? You know you're welcome any time, Marion. Fran particularly said to tell you.'

'I'll remember. Thanks.' And this time her pride wouldn't stop her.

'In fact, what about joining us for lunch this Sunday? If you're free?'

'Well, yes, I'm free . . .'

'Then please do!' He allowed his eyes to do the persuading.

She smiled. 'All right, thanks, I'd love to. It'll be great to see them again and perhaps . . .' she faltered, 'perhaps I could have another look at Rebecca's special book. I didn't have a proper chance last time.'

'I think that's an excellent idea.' Its significance was not lost on Denham, either. 'I'll get Fran to give you a ring. Now, will you be okay from here? I really must get back.'

'I'll be fine, thanks, Den.'

'Goodbye, then, Marion. And God bless.'

With a wave, he left her—cassock flowing, unruly fair hair stirring in the breeze. A remarkable member of a remarkable family. However all this was destined to end, she was proud to have been linked with them.

CHAPTER TEN

THE carol concert was a success. The hall looked charming, the choir sang sweetly, the instrumentalists played with panache if not strict accuracy. The children were proud and their audience of parents, friends and relations were rapt.

Rebecca tootled her recorder in several groups as well as her solo, joining the choir the rest of the time. She was so radiant, basking in the limelight and the fact that her aunt and uncle, complete with wriggling (but mercifully mainly silent) cousins, had come specially to witness her moment of glory. She was a transformed child.

And of course jumping with excitement because her father would soon be here. Christmas was only round the corner, so it couldn't be long now, could it? Every day she pointed this out to Marion, and no doubt to Fran or Den too. Every day it became more agonisingly hard to nod, ruffle those dark-gold curls and affectionately agree. Another two days—three at the most—and Rebecca would have to be warned, at least prepared for the strong possibility that he was unlikely to make it back in time. If nothing worse.

Now Marion sat with those of her class who were not in the choir or orchestra, smiling at parents, waving across to Fran and Den, leaning to catch a whispered comment from a pupil. Generally, she enjoyed these events. Treble voices warbling familiar little melodies: *Away in a Manger*, *Once in Royal David's City*. The sound usually pricked tears of pleasurable sentiment at the back of her eyes. And the choir's renditions of more obscure seasonal songs; today they were singing *The Cowboy Carol*, *Whence is that Goodly Fragrance Flowing*, and a French one, *Il est Né, le Divin Enfant*, in which Rebecca was notable for her confident fluency. Then standing to join in the old favourites, *The First Noël*, *While Shepherds Watched* . . . yes, she often felt a contented glow at this time of year, however much she grumbled about it.

But today it was all a pretence, and at its centre an aching dark void. How could she concentrate on anything, still less enjoy it, in the bleak knowledge that Nicol lay severely injured, probably unconscious, thousands of miles away? Over two weeks had dragged by and still there was no substantial news. Via the American publisher, Den had succeeded in gleaning a few titbits of information: the likely whereabouts of the archaeological project, the possible location of the hospital. But exact details, names— even confirmation of what they knew already—were elusive and vague. Communications were evidently worse that ever, by virtue of the fact that a severe hurricane had recently battered the shores all the way down the Gulf of Mexico. In a country fraught with natural disasters, enquiries into the fate of one man in an extremely remote area were simply ignored or lost.

Den was becoming exasperated. If it went on any longer, he was going to have to fly out there himself and see if he could get any closer to the facts, or to his brother, in person. But there was little spare cash around, and Fran was far from keen on the idea. Bad enough losing Nicol without risking Den too. Perhaps she had a point, but it was frustrating and distressing all the same.

Meanwhile, true to his word, he kept Marion in

the picture—such as it was. Most evenings, with Rebecca safely in bed, either he or Fran would telephone her to exchange mutual encouragement. It was good to know they were there, but in the end she was on her own; especially through the endless black nights, when this emptiness swelled to a craving—the nagging urge to see Nicol, hear him, touch him . . . and to fill in those gaps, smooth out the ragged edges cruelly left in a relationship which had barely blossomed.

Time. They had needed so much time, and now it seemed their clock had stopped before it had really started to tick. For all Marion knew, Nic was dead. There was always hope, but on the other side of that coin there was always despair.

Mechanically, she chatted and laughed as she waved her pupils off.

"Bye, Miss! Have a nice holiday, Miss! See you next term . . . Happy Christmas, Happy Christmas, Miss . . .!'

Wearily she tidied up the classroom one last time, then collected her belongings and went through it all again with her colleagues:

'Cheers then, Marion! Take care! Enjoy yourself, don't drink too much, don't do anything I wouldn't . . . Happy Christmas, Happy Christmas . . .!'

Then she plodded home through the afternoon dusk, laden with books, files, and the perennial stacks of cards: robins, holly, mistletoe; neat unformed messages of genuine goodwill. Thank goodness for the children. What was she going to do without them now?

She must think positive. Two days to recover, including a third Sunday at the vicarage—linchpins of this past dreadful fortnight. Then up to Shropshire for the family festivities. It would be a strain, because she'd told them next to nothing; but it might be good

to get away . . . try to relax. It might be. If she told
herself than often enough, she might even believe it.

Her flat would be dark and empty, but the central
heating would be on so she could have a bath, make
herself eat a bit of supper, settle in front of some
mindless, numbing drivel on the small screen.

She approached the house, fumbling in the chaos
of her bag for her keys. Climbing the four broad
steps to the front door, she mechanically reached for
the lock—and jumped back with a gasp, as a figure
moved out of the shadows and into the dim light of
the porch.

A mugger! A rapist, lying in wait for unsuspecting
victims as they arrived home! Streetwise citizen of a
violent world, Marion reacted on a reflex. She
dropped everything but her tough plastic briefcase,
lifted it as high as she could, poised to bring it
heavily down on any handy portion of his anatomy.
The more vulnerable, the better. No marauder was
going to get away with confronting her, at the
entrance of her own home, not without a healthy
struggle . . .

But he was much too fast for her, and caught both
her wrists in a tough grip so that the case slithered
uselessly to the ground, landing on her big toe and
causing her to hop on the other foot, swearing in a
highly unladylike fashion.

'May I book this next dance?' The villain's deep
tones were vibrant with humour but distinctly low on
menace. 'We really shouldn't go on meeting like this,'
he added, for good measure.

Marion stared, eyes and mouth wide open, even
less ladylike. Then she was sobbing and giggling on
the same breath, seized by a wave of hysteria for the
first time in her life.

'Nicol! Oh, Nicol!'

'Hallo, Marion.'

The pain in her toe was transient. Even the ache in her heart could vanish magically, on the instant. But registering this miracle was one thing; finding words in the face of it, quite another.

'What . . . how . . . when?' she gabbled foolishly.

He was still grasping her wrists. Now he drew her to him, and details crept through to her dazed brain. A jagged slash, healed but still angry red, the length of his right cheek. Faint purple bruising around his right eye, and across temple and forehead. Closely cropped hair—the fine gold-brown mane reduced to an uncharacteristic short back and sides, with one patch behind his ear shaved even closer. Cuts and contusions on the rest of his face. And the relatively inconsequential fact that his glasses were cracked across one lens, the bridge held together with sticking plaster.

He released her hands. At once she reached up to touch him; tentative fingertips tracing the contours of his face, the loved and remembered planes and hollows of cheekbones, nose, chin . . . then, very softly, the hateful weals on his flesh. Even as she clenched with anxious pity at the wounds, she marvelled at the warmth of his skin, the solidity of his frame, despite the fact that he was thinner. Of course he would be physically depleted; but he was alive, and upright, and the acute blue of his eyes was undiminished. And above all, he was here!

For half a minute he stood, passively allowing the contact. Then his patience wore out and he gathered her against him, crushing her to his chest in arms that had lost none of their power. His chin nuzzled her face, two days' growth of beard rasping on the softness of the cheeks and brow. Muttered words were lost among the silken strands of her hair, but it made no difference. Tears poured down Marion's face, choking her own voice back. Time enough for words, later.

Marion never remembered it, but they must have picked up her scattered possessions, as well as his suitcase, and stumbled upstairs to her flat. Safely there, she drew him down beside her on the sofa. The reality of his presence was still uncertain. She had to drink it in, study him properly, here in this better light, in private.

He was pale, under a striking tan. New lines—stress, pain, exhaustion—mapped the skin round eyes and mouth. He had been severely traumatised, but he was in no way dwindled. If anything he was enhanced, the experience of suffering lending an extra strength.

Marion simply went on gazing, recalling each familiar crease, already welcoming new ones. And while she did so, though she barely noticed, Nicol was doing the same to her.

His hands clasped her head, tilting it back. 'You look different. Just as lovely, but changed.' He frowned, lips compressing. 'You've been very unhappy. Because of me? I'm sorry.'

She was moved—that he should apologise. Next to what he'd been through, her own agitation faded. 'Don't be sorry. Just be glad you're here. It was all worth it, as long as you're here.'

She knew his smile so well—had tried, yet failed, to envisage it so often during those lonely nights. Now it sent shivers up her spine and kindled embers at the core of her.

'I'm here. You think I'd let them keep me away from you?' Still cupping her face between both hands, he leaned closer to kiss her lightly on the cheek, nose, lips. She had been dreading never to feel that touch again; now it sent miniature explosions through her, swept her breath clean away. She shut her eyes, relishing it.

When he drew back, he stared down into her eyes and smiled again. 'So—you got my telegram?'

Pulled back to earth, Marion forced herself to some kind of lucidity. This was perfect—incredible— but bewildering too. 'What telegram?'

'The one I sent, to tell you I'd been unavoidably detained, but I was all right and would be home as soon as I could.'

'No.' She stared back at him. 'Nothing like that. All we knew was—about your accident, and that you were . . .' She winced.

'I was what?' He was sharp, leaning forward. 'What, Marion?'

'Unconscious. In hospital. Badly hurt.'

Now it was his turn to be bewildered. 'You knew all that? When?'

She shook her head. 'Oh, I don't know—ages ago—too long ago.' With an effort, she worked it out. Did all this really matter? 'The beginning of this month. Den had a call from your publishers.'

'You mean, you all knew I'd had the crash, all that time ago, but not that I was okay?' He clutched his brow. 'Good God, that bloody country! The one time I *didn't* want a message sent, they got one through and never even told me they'd done it. Then, when I specifically asked them to, they obviously didn't manage it.' He groaned.

'When—when did you send the second message?'

'As far as I was concerned, the *only* message,' he corrected grimly. 'Let me see—must have been ten days ago. As soon as I was able to think straight. Remembered where I was . . . where I should have been,' he added, with a sardonic glance into her face.

'But you were unconscious? Before that?'

'Oh yes.' The grimness tightened, 'I was—for three

days. Then, when I came round, I couldn't remember much. Gradually it all came back, and I realised I had to get in touch with you right away. All of you—but especially you, Marion. The others weren't expecting to hear from me, but you . . .' he broke off, biting his lip. Then he was leaning towards her again, his expression fraught. 'Marion, you did get my letter?

'I did.' She met his gaze steadily. 'And I went to Banbridge.'

'You did.' He repeated it, deadpan, nodding slowly. 'Of course you did. My poor sweet! You must have suffered. What a fiasco! Talk about bathos! It must have been one of the lowlights of your life. I must have been your least favourite person.'

Marion even managed a small smile. 'It wasn't too good, at the time. But I got over it. In fact . . .' she hesitated, 'in a strange way, it was quite beneficial. In the end . . . I can't explain . . .'

'I intended to be there. I was all set to come. You know that, don't you, Marion?' He took her hand, pressing it. 'Don't you?'

'I do now; yes.'

Nicol studied her with a deep interest, laced with admiration. 'It's not a bad place, is it? The Swan?'

'It's a beautiful place, as you well know. And nice people, too.'

'Yes. I always meant to go again, when the occasion arose.'

She could almost swear he was teasing her. 'And it arose with me.'

'So I thought. So I thought, Marion.' He sighed.

'Nic . . .?' He still had hold of her hand, more loosely now.

'Yes, Marion?'

'Who did you go with, last time you were there?'

'Oh, it was years ago. I went with a lady friend.'

'Just a friend? She couldn't prevent herself, she had to know.

'Well . . .' he considered. 'No, perhaps friend isn't quite the word. She was more than a friend, but less than one too. Less—permanent. More of a passing fancy.'

'I see.' Marion was curiously stiff. 'And do you always entertain your passing fancies there?'

'All the time.' He dropped the frivolity. 'No, I've only been there the once. As I said, it was a long time ago, but I've heard good reports of it since, and I though it would be ideal for . . .' he shrugged.

'I did wonder,' she ventured, cautious but determined to see it out, 'if you'd been there with Andrea?'

'Andrea?' He frowned. 'No, she never even knew I went.'

Marion's eyes widened. 'You mean, you were married at the time?'

'Oh yes. If you can use the word.' His gaze was fixed on the middle distance; abruptly he transferred it back to her. 'Listen, I'll tell you about that; I've got plenty to say on that subject. It's what I kept putting off before I went. And if you never got my wire, it looks as if I've got plenty to tell you about all this lot, too . . .' He indicated his cuts and bruises. 'But first, Marion, I have a favour to ask.'

'Anything. You know that.' She gazed at him anxiously.

'Make me a cup of hot, strong coffee. Preferably two. And maybe a sandwich? I've come here straight from the airport. The last bit of nourishment I got was made of the same PVC as its container. In fact, I rather think I might have eaten the container as well.'

'Oh Nic, I'm so sorry. You must be so tired, and . . . how could I . . .? Oh God, I'm sorry!' Marion was on her feet, palms pressed to burning cheeks, remorse cutting a swathe through all those other emotions—delight and amazement and the slow reawakening of passion.

He leaned back, grinning at her confusion. 'Ah, this is what I've missed! The personal attentions of a good woman. Those nurses were very fine, but no one flames and glows like you do, Marion.'

'No one?'

'No one in the world,' he assured her.

'Wait there. Make yourself comfortable. Have a shower—a wash. Have a rest. Do what you like. I won't be a minute.'

She was all flustered, in this urgency to care for him, enfold him, never let him be hurt again. At the same time, she needed him, yearned hungrily, helplessly for him. It was a new, profound conflict, and it paralysed her.

'All at once? Or one at a time?' He sat forward, watching her, elbows on knees, brows slightly quirked.

'Oh, you know what I mean. I—I won't be long.' Blushing at her own ineptness and his affectionate irony, she fled to the kitchen.

An hour later, Nicol was washed and refreshed, and they were both fortified with soup, home-made pizza from the freezer, a packet of shortbread, fruit and coffee. He stretched expansively, settling into his corner of the sofa, and beamed at her.

'Now, where were we? That's better. I can face the inquisition.'

'Why don't you just tell me everything, starting with the crash,' Marion suggested, leaning back and folding her arms.

He launched in without preamble. 'The problem with the crash was not so much its seriousness, as the fact that I was out on a full day's trek and no one knew exactly where I was. Thank God I was near a road when it happened, and a passing truck spotted me, otherwise there's no knowing how long I'd have lain there.' He shuddered, and so did Marion. His colour had returned, with food and rest, but now it drained again. She held out a concerned hand to him.

'You needn't tell me any of this now, you know. Maybe you'd rather just put your feet up . . go to bed . . .'

'Bed?' His brows arched. 'My dear lady, I appreciate the invitation, but I can't guarantee my stamina at this juncture, what with jet-lag and . . .'

Her skin suffused, a tidal wave of embarrassment. Was it her own Freudian slip, or his mischievous interpretation? Or both? 'That wasn't what I meant, and you know it!'

'I beg your pardon. My mistake.'

'So get on with this story and behave yourself.'

'Yes, Miss. Sorry, Miss. As I was saying, these injuries were pretty nasty, but the main problem was that I was concussed. Well out of it, for quite a while. A most extraordinary experience, Marion. I don't recommend it—or at least, the coming round bit at the end.'

'But where were you? Where was the hospital?'

'Oh, it was a makeshift affair. A remote little township in the back of beyond. But they were very good to me,' he mused, absently fingering his scars, his gaze focusing away on to recent vague memories.

'They looked after you? The treatment was all right?'

'On the primitive side, but quite okay as long as no complications set in, which fortunately they didn't. I think they relied on a wish and a prayer, more than modern refinements of medicine or surgery. Most of them were nuns, ministering angels. I suspect they took one look at me and recognised the sheer resilience of my constitution. It's taken some bashes in its time. I expect they were wise enough to realise it would be spared to take a few more if they left well alone.'

He made it sound ludicrously simple. 'Pity *we* weren't wise enough to realise that,' Marion remarked drily.

It was meant to be an aside, but it distracted Nicol from his theme. 'Good lord, yes: I was forgetting, you knew all about it, much earlier than I realised! Thanks to someone's efficiency. Let me see . . .' he was deeply intent, brows knitted. 'Most have been those people at the dig, sending a message to the publishers in Mexico City—no doubt they thought they were doing me a big favour.' He shook his head at the irony of it. 'What exactly did you hear, Marion?'

'That you had a fractured skull and were in a coma.'

'God! You must have been frantic!'

'Something like that.' Self-protection from the memory was setting in already, as it faded into a misty, murky recent past.

'It was gross exaggeration. The impact knocked me out, yes, and it took about a week before my faculties really cleared themselves. When they did, I asked the Sister to organise a message to you—so you wouldn't worry.' He clicked his tongue in sardonic irritation. 'They swore they had. Another case of *mañana*, I suppose.'

'And there were no other injuries? Internal ones?'

'No. I was dead lucky. Shocked, shaken, in need of patching up. The moment I was on my feet, I discharged myself and headed for the nearest airport. I knew you were expecting me. I couldn't let you down . . . any of you . . . including Becky, of course . . .' Suddenly he was banging his forehead with a clenched fist. 'Hey, I've just thought! I'm a crass idiot! Why didn't I . . . if Becky knew all this—

and you never had that second message—she must be worried sick! I'd better get straight round there, or at least phone to say I'm okay . . .'

'Of course you should. But don't worry about Becky.' Marion was quick to reassure him. 'We didn't tell her, Nic. We decided not to until . . . we were waiting till just before Christmas, then we were going to have to say something,' she concluded, a lot more lamely than she had started, as the prospect hit her all over again. Thank God it wouldn't be necessary, after all!

'Thank God for that!' Echoing her thoughts, Nicol slumped, pale again with relief. 'Bad enough to imagine you, and Den and Fran, only knowing the worst, and no more . . . But Becky . . .' he cringed. Then he reached over to grab her hand. 'Thanks, Marion. I'll make it up to you, I promise. Just—thanks.'

'It wasn't only me,' she reminded him. 'Den and Fran were as worried as I was, even though . . .'

'Though they hadn't been stood up and left on tenterhooks?'

'I didn't even mention that to them, actually. But they were very good to me, Nic. They're marvellous people. I really like them.'

'I'm quite sure the feeling's mutual.'

They studied one another; their eyes seemed threaded, on a beam of light. Marion attempted, unsuccessfully, to break away from it. 'Do you think you ought to go round there now?' she murmured, prompted more by a sense of duty than any wish to lose sight of him.

'I'm sure I ought.' But he was pulling her towards him, inexorably into the warmth of his body, until she lay across his lap. Then he was kissing her, with a profound, lingering tenderness. After a very long time, when he had quite finished, he muttered,

'You're dead right, of course. I ought to at least phone them. Now.'

But he kissed her again, and this time the contact ripened, deepened. She was dry matchwood, set alight. Channels opened, pulsated all the way through her. That ache of longing sharpened to desire, now he was actually here at last, in her arms; so many bittersweet hopes and fears embodied in this fusion, this moment.

His hands explored her face, then her neck, shoulders, arms; under her clothes they searched for the soft curves of her breasts, waist, stomach, hips, thighs. In her turn she strained to him, revelling in the sensuality—the hard fact of him, as her hands ranged freely over sinew and muscle, bone and skin, restoring fantasy to flesh.

The friction rose, generating heat, gathering its own impetus. In a final, half-hearted bid for common sense, Marion prised herself away, eyeing him coyly. 'What about your poor wilting stamina?'

'It appears to have miraculously returned,' he growled. Then he pulled her back into his arms, and set about providing incontrovertible proof. Thoroughly, and deliciously, until the shock waves rose and spread, wave after wave, gasp upon gasp, sweeter, yet more shattering than ever.

Afterwards he held her very close, for timeless, thoughtless minutes. Finally she shifted free from where she was wedged, between his body and the back of the sofa. Lying on top of him, she gazed down into his face, which was as transfigured as her own must surely be—lit from within. Infinitely careful, agonisingly tender, she touched the wounds, the bruises, traced the raw scars with a gentle fingertip. Nicol opened his eyes and smiled up at her, and she smiled back. 'Does it hurt?'

'Not really. Even at the time it wasn't too bad. It

seemed to happen in slow motion—yet so fast I didn't really feel it.' Oddly objective, he reflected. 'As if another person was driving that jeep and I was just watching the whole thing. Weird business.'

'But you're really all right now? Really better enough to be here?'

He made a wry face at her. 'What do you think?'

'Oh, Nicol!' She buried her face in his neck, her hair flowing across his chest, her arms round him, tight, tight, defending them both from that gruesome image; the one which had haunted her nightmares—waking and sleeping—for so long. 'I've missed you so much . . . wanted you . . . I was afraid I'd never . . .'

It was his turn to pluck her off him, so that he could see into her eyes. His own were deeply serious. 'And you've forgiven me for all the rest? For not being honest with you, before I left?'

'Oh, that.' From the security of here and now, it felt paltry. 'I forgave you almost at once. I can see how difficult it was for you.'

'I was a damn fool, not to tell you earlier. I don't usually have trouble finding words, Marion. This time I just couldn't seem to get the right ones out at the right moment. So Becky had to take over. The poor kid was desperate to let you know, and I kept saying I'd tell you, and forbidding her to do it . . . but she was right. She knew you should be told, as soon as possible. She was right, and I was wrong.'

He had darkened with tense guilt, and Marion refused to let discord into this harmony. 'Hey, it's okay. It's really all right. I'm fine, and she's fine. Everything turned out fine. Don't worry. It can't be good for you,' she added, with a twinge of concern.

He rolled over, taking charge, staring down at her. 'I've got to tell you more about it now, though, Marion. Before we can go on, I've got to go back. Can you take it?'

'If *you* can.' Anything, to keep him so close, his body welded to hers, all the way down; keep this contact, for ever.

'I told you, my stamina is fully restored, You're the ultimate health cure.' As if for further invigoration, he hugged her. 'It's about Andrea. As you've gathered, she looked quite like you.'

'More than quite, from what I could see in those photos.'

'Well, maybe. But what I'm trying to tell you is this. There is a similarity, yes. But at the same time, there isn't.'

'You mean it's only skin deep?' She had to help him out. It was so rare to see him groping painfully for expressive words.

'That's just it. I knew you'd understand.'

'It's not so difficult, Nicol. Den mentioned it, and . . .'

'Den's talked to you about it?' He seemed startled, though not upset.

'Once, in passing. Nothing much, just that the resemblance was strictly superficial. He said you'd want to tell me the rest yourself.'

Nicol had slithered round so that they both lay on their sides, faces close. 'He's no fool, my brother. So you'll appreciate how much of a shock it was, meeting you for the first time. But once I got to know you, I realised you were a totally different type of woman from Andrea. All the same, this physical thing was a bit uncanny. And Becky had already been so struck by it, at school . . .'

'I know. She kept following me around and staring at me.'

'Well, yes, she would. But I'm sure that now she sees you as an individual, in your own right. Nothing to do with her mother. She just wanted it cleared up, out of the way—and so did I, but . . .' Nicol drew in a long breath and expelled it on a sigh. 'You see, it's like this, Marion. Andrea and I were not happy. She was a—a hopeless case. I began to see it, almost as soon as we were married. She was lively and pretty and fun; clever too, in her way. But trivial—and pathologically fickle. Promiscuous.'

He laid it on the line, unsparing of himself, or Marion, or the memory of his wife. 'Fidelity was an alien concept to her. She didn't know the meaning of the word. If ever two people should have had a simple affair and left it at that, it was Andrea and me.' He sighed again. 'There was a string of other men, incessantly, wherever we went. She used to say it was the only way she could keep the domestic scene going—the extramural excitements added that necessary zing—all that nonsense,' he concluded bitterly.

'I'm sorry, Nic.' It was a clear echo, back to that earlier time: that earlier conversation (a hundred years ago? a month? two?) when she had told him about John Wood, and his use of her as a prop to a failing marriage. The spice that allowed the old habits to continue . . .

'I believe in commitment, and she didn't. That's the long and short of it, Marion. I know you sometimes have to work hard to keep a relationship alive. For years, I tried everything: cajoling, seduction, rage. I thought perhaps, after Becky . . . but that just made things worse. We hardly even saw her, the baby and I. When we did, she always insisted she loved us both and we weren't to take her little peccadilloes seriously, but of course we did.'

'Of course.' There wasn't much Marion could say, but she was absorbing every word, even as she prayed that reliving it wouldn't distress him too much. He was right: it was vital she should know.

'So, anyway, in Hong Kong, when she—when she

drowned . . .' He paused, then rallied. 'She was on that launch with just one other person—her current lover. A prosperous businessman, German, I think. It was his boat, and they were enjoying an intimate little voyage round the islands, *à deux*. Which turned out to be their last.'

'Oh, Nicol!' The sympathy in her eyes mirrored the recalled pain in his. 'And I bet you blamed yourself for all this.'

'Too bloody right I did! Even when she died. For some crazy reason, I blamed myself for that as well.'

'Well, you were wrong, and you musn't—not any more. It wasn't your responsibility. You must draw a line under all that, start again.' Marion was utterly sure she was right, and the certainty showed in her face and voice. 'Remember what you wrote to me, Nic? *Shadows of your own making*. And . . .' she grinned then, just a little wickedly, 'I know what they say about men being attracted to particular types of women. I may look like Andrea, but I assure you, here and now, that's as far as it goes. From what you've told me, I'm opposite in every other way.'

'I should never have doubted it. But perhaps you can see why my reactions to you were decidedly— shall we say mixed?'

'I can—now. When I first found out, I thought you were using me as—I don't know—some kind of cheap substitute. The next best thing, since you'd lost the real one.'

'That was why I should have tackled the subject with you much sooner. *Mea culpa*. I was in a state of confusion. Here I was, apparently about to repeat my worst mistakes by falling in love with the same woman twice . . . then when I realised you were light years from being the same woman—well, it was too late; I couldn't find a convincing way to break it to you.'

'It's not too late, Nic.' Marion ran her fingers

across his cropped head. She preferred the hair longer, but there was a new tactile quality, even something erotic, about the smooth brush of it against her palms. 'Nic?' she murmured.

'Yes, my sweet girl?' He was relaxed, the truth wrung out of him at last.

'Did you really fall in love with me?'

'Oh yes, I did. I have. I am. I never stopped dreaming of you—longing for you—all the time I was away. Even when I was unconscious, I'm pretty sure you were there somewhere, calling me back.'

'And do you really believe in being committed?'

'Definitely. Always have.' Spotting her quizzical look, he grinned. 'You're thinking of my passing fancy, aren't you?'

'I might be.'

'It was the only time. Just when things were at rock bottom between Andrea and me. It was a kind of—furious despair. The girl meant nothing to me, or vice versa, I can swear to that, Marion. I'm only human, and our marriage was in little else but name. Andrea was free with her favours, as long as she was free of emotional ties with the men concerned. As soon as there was a question of that, she went off them. Not surprisingly, she went off me, early on in the proceedings. About a week after we got hitched, to be precise. Not much I could do about it then, but I told you, I was fond of her and I kept trying.'

'I'm glad you've told me. And I don't mind about the lady at the Swan. I'm broad-minded; a woman of the world.'

'So it'll be all right if I do the same again, in future?'

She pretended to consider—though the very idea made her curl up inside with jealousy. 'If you do it when you're with me, even once, I shall never speak to you again,' she announced coolly. 'But,' she added, snuggling up to him, 'I'll make sure you never need to.'

'And if I ask you to marry me, you won't get bored? Go off me?'

Bored? With Nicol Jarvis! Not if she lived with him ninety years!

But Marion wasn't without a few female wiles, and now she gazed at him from under her lashes. 'I'm not making any rash promises; you'll have to try it out and see.'

'Oh, I get it. You want me down there, on one knee.' Nicol waved a hand at the floor. 'Grovelling at your feet. After all my troubles?'

'That's right.'

He thought about it, but didn't move a muscle. 'I'll tell you what I'm going to do, Marion. Listen carefully.'

'I'm listening.'

'I'm going to stick around here for a long, long time. I'm going to write up my Mexico book, and it'll be another best-seller. Then I'm going to take up an offer of a lectureship at the University which has been pending for years. They'll be pleased to capture me at last,' he observed, without false modesty.

'You're not going to travel any more? Why not?'

'I've had a bellyful. I need to settle down. If and when I take to the road again, it'll be a long way ahead—and with the full approval of all the women in my life. Whoever they may be.'

'But where will you live?'

'I've got my eye on a rather dignified residence that's for sale, not far from the vicarage. One of those pretty Georgian terraced houses with the flat fronts. You know where I mean? I sussed it out before I left. I'm planning to buy it, Marion.'

'Oh, Nic! Becky will be so thrilled!' It was an irrational response, hardly expressing her own dawning exhilaration, but they both knew it implied more than the mere words suggested.

'I hope so. And it'll take the pressure off Den and Fran, though I'm sure Fran will go on lending a hand. But what about you, Marion?'

'What about me?'

'Are you pleased? Do you like the idea?'

It sounded like heaven on earth: her eyes gleamed their message, belying her measured reply. 'I'm not averse to it. I'd say it has a fair bit going for it.'

He chuckled. 'And when I've got it under way . . . when it looks as if I might have a home base and a steady job and all the trimmings . . .'

'You don't need a steady job!' she interrupted indignantly. '*I've* got one!' Then she flushed because she had given herself away.

Nicol grinned broadly. 'I know that, Miss. But what if you decide to take a bit of time off? A well-earned rest, or . . .' his glance grew sly, 'a spot of maternity leave?'

'You could take paternity leave!' But he had made his point, and the delight glowed now, incandescent in her face.

'I could. I've done my share of child-minding, don't forget. I enjoy it. I'll do as much as you like. Best thing is to share in both—outside work, domestic duties. As a teacher, don't you agree?'

'As a matter of fact, I do.' Marion had never applied the dictum to herself; now she did, and she liked it all the more.

'So.' He sat upright, brisk. 'I reserve the down-on-one-knee performance for later. When I've made some arrangements, and of course consulted the other female I adore. But you've had due warning of my intentions. So, what do you say, Miss Thomas?'

She disliked the cold draught of air that lapped around her naked self, now that he had moved away.

She held out her arms to him, and at once he came into them again. 'What do you say, Marion?' he muttered, against her mouth. 'Do you believe in the value of a lifelong commitment? Or are you a modern self-contained entity, wed to your career, or your independence?'

'I value fidelity, and I love you. You can safely skip the proposal scene, Nic. Spare your creaking joints. The answer will be yes. Yes, please, Nicol. To all of it.'

'That's good. I don't think I could have stood the suspense.'

For some minutes there was complete silence. Then she broke from his embrace just far enough to whisper, 'Do you think Becky will mind?'

'Becky?' His eyes were glazed, his lips still parted, close to hers.

'Rebecca. Your daughter, you know, the one who . . .'

'I suspect she'll be bowled over. She loves you already, you know that. I suspect it'll be the best Christmas present she could have. Mind you, I also suspect it'll be a long time before she gets round to using your name, instead of Miss.'

Their smiles infected one another, and reflected off one another. They were an enclosed unit, two in one.

Then Nicol said, 'Talking of Christmas presents— one more thing I've got to ask you. To add to my scenario, but in the shorter term.'

'Oh yes? The shorter term?' Marion mocked the formal phrase.

'I imagine we're both pledged to spend the festive season in the bosom of our respective families. But what about New Year?'

'Yes, I'd better go up there, try and explain about all this . . . but I'm free at New Year. Why? What do you have in mind?'

'What I have in mind is an exorcism. Of your frustrations, as well as mine. A wiping of the slate; a turning of the new leaf.'

'What do you mean?' Marion was puzzled.

'I mean, I want you to spend the turn of the year with me, at the Swan Inn, Banbridge. Just the two of us. A sinful, peaceful, wonderful week. How about it, Marion?'

She needed no persuading: none at all. No suggestion could have been more welcome, or more perfect. 'I'll come. As long as we travel there together. I'm not sitting around, waiting for you!'

'Understood. Luxury transport will be provided.'

'Left-hand drive, of course.'

'I'm not so sure. I'll be buying my own car this time, and maybe it ought to be more conventional. In case you ever want some lessons.'

She laughed. 'That's looking ahead a bit. Perhaps one day.'

'House, car, family roots. What am I getting into?' Nicol shook his head ruefully. Then suddenly he was galvanised into action, grabbing her hands, pulling her up to stand beside him. 'This isn't good enough. It really won't do. Talking of families—I must get round to mine, break all this good news. They won't know what's hit them. I keep forgetting they don't even know I'm back in the country.'

'They don't even know you're alive and well,' Marion reminded him quietly, holding his hands tighter as if to confirm it.

'Except Becky. But I should get there and see her now, even so.'

'Of course you should.'

'You'll come with me, won't you, Marion?'

'If you want me to, Nic.'

'I'll always want you to.' He kissed her, then

murmured, 'And I'll always want you. *You*; not a ghost, or a shadow. Always.'

'I know that. And I'll always want you.' She returned his kiss with such ardency, his own passion threatened to engulf them both. Eventually, reluctantly, he broke away.

'Come on, my precious girl. We've got plenty of time for all this. All the time in the world.'

It was a misunderstanding that could cost a young woman her virtue, and a notorious rake his heart.

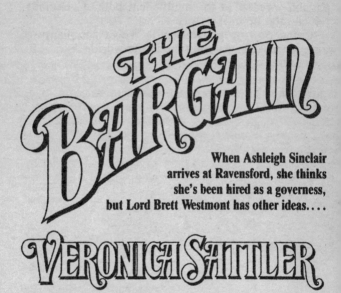

THE BARGAIN

When Ashleigh Sinclair
arrives at Ravensford, she thinks
she's been hired as a governess,
but Lord Brett Westmont has other ideas....

VERONICA SATTLER

ATTRACTIVE, SPACE SAVING BOOK RACK

Display your most prized novels on this handsome and sturdy book rack. The hand-rubbed walnut finish will blend into your library decor with quiet elegance, providing a practical organizer for your favorite hard-or softcovered books.

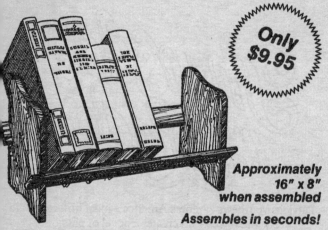

Only $9.95

Approximately 16" x 8" when assembled

Assembles in seconds!

To order, rush your name, address and zip code, along with a check or money order for $10.70* ($9.95 plus 75¢ postage and handling) payable to *Harlequin Reader Service*:

Harlequin Reader Service
Book Rack Offer
901 Fuhrmann Blvd.
P.O. Box 1396
Buffalo, NY 14269-1396

Offer not available in Canada.

*New York and Iowa residents add appropriate sales tax.

BKR-1A

For the millions who can't read
Give the Gift of Literacy

One out of five adults in North America
cannot read or write well enough
to fill out a job application
or understand the directions on a bottle of medicine.

**You can change all this by joining the fight
against illiteracy.**

For more information write to:
Contact, Box 81826, Lincoln, Neb. 68501
In the United States, call toll free: 1-800-228-8813

**The only degree you need
is a degree of caring**

Six exciting series for you every month... from Harlequin

Harlequin Romance·
The series that started it all

Tender, captivating and heartwarming...
love stories that sweep you off to faraway places
and delight you with the magic of love.

◆

Harlequin Presents·
Powerful contemporary love stories...as individual as the women who read them

The No. 1 romance series...
exciting love stories for you, the woman of today...
a rare blend of passion and dramatic realism.

◆

Harlequin Superromance®
It's more than romance...
it's Harlequin Superromance

A sophisticated, contemporary romance-fiction
series, providing you with a longer,
more involving read...a richer mix of complex plots,
realism and adventure.

Harlequin
American Romance™
Harlequin celebrates the American woman...

...by offering you romance stories written about American women, by American women for American women. This series offers you contemporary romances uniquely North American in flavor and appeal.

◆

Harlequin Temptation
Passionate stories for today's woman

An exciting series of sensual, mature stories of love...dilemmas, choices, resolutions... all contemporary issues dealt with in a true-to-life fashion by some of your favorite authors.

◆

Harlequin Intrigue
Because romance can be quite an adventure

Harlequin Intrigue, an innovative series that blends the romance you expect... with the unexpected. Each story has an added element of intrigue that provides a new twist to the Harlequin tradition of romance excellence.

Harlequin Books·

PROD-A-2

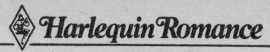
◈ Harlequin Romance

Coming Next Month

Available in December wherever paperback books are sold,
or through Harlequin Reader Service.

In the U.S.
901 Fuhrmann Blvd.
P.O. Box 1397
Buffalo, N.Y. 14240-1397

In Canada
P.O. Box 603
Fort Erie, Ontario
L2A 5X3